JOURNEY

TIANA PADGETT-GRANT

CLAY BRIDGES
PRESS

Journey
Copyright © 2025 by Tiana Padgett-Grant
Illustrated by Illustrator Name
Photography by Photographer Name

Published by Clay Bridges Press in Houston, TX
www.ClayBridgesPress.com

Unless otherwise indicated, scripture quotations are taken from the ESV® Bible (The Holy Bible, English Standard Version®), copyright © 2001 by Crossway, a publishing ministry of Good News Publishers. Used by permission. All rights reserved.

ISBN: 978-1-68488-140-6
eISBN: 978-1-68488-141-3

Special Sales: Most Clay Bridges titles are available in special quantity discounts. Custom imprinting or excerpting can also be done to fit special needs. Contact Clay Bridges at Info@ClayBridgesPress.com

SPECIAL THANKS

I want to thank my Heavenly Father for being the Author of my life and the source of my strength. Without His grace and guidance, this story would not exist.

To my incredible family: Thank you for standing beside me with love, patience, and encouragement as I poured my heart into this project. Your support means more than words can say.

And to you, dear reader: Thank you for picking up this book. My prayer is that these pages remind you to trust that even in seasons of brokenness, God is near, working in ways you may not yet see.

TABLE OF CONTENTS

CHAPTER 1

Alone in her penthouse apartment, Journey was in total despair as she looked at her reflection in the bathroom mirror. The bathroom floor was stained with her blood, and the tiles felt cold.

Her reflection looked like a person with whom she was not familiar. Was this the face of someone who was barren—someone who could not carry a fetus to term?

This was Journey's second miscarriage, and no one could have prepared her for this moment. This was her moment of shame and pain. She struggled to control the emotions of complete sadness and emptiness. Journey questioned God, asking why she didn't deserve the title of mother.

She heard a knock at the bathroom door, which startled her because she thought she was alone in the apartment. Journey pulled herself together, wiping the mascara and melted makeup from her face.

She put on her Hollywood tone and said, "Hey! Who is it?"

"Babe, it's me. Are you okay?"

Oh snap, I forgot Lance was coming back from Florida tonight.

She didn't want to tell him what had just happened. It would break him even more than the last time. Lance always talked about how much he wanted to be a father, and she wanted to give him that.

"Hey, yeah! I'm fine! Uh. I am about to get in the shower," she explained.

Lance said in a sweet tone, "Oh, okay. I thought I heard you crying. But be quick, babe! I missed you."

When she heard him say, "I missed you," she knew what that meant. He wanted to have sex. Any other night, she would be down for it, but she didn't think her body could take anything going inside after all that had just come out of it. Journey had to think of an excuse.

She shouted, "Not tonight, babe. I have my period!"

After she cleaned up the mess and herself, she walked out of the bathroom into the living room, which had bright fluorescent lights and pearl-white walls. She saw Lance on the couch watching TV. Journey studied him as if she were seeing him for the first time.

His long legs were draped over the divan by the window. Although he was too tall to fit comfortably on that couch, he loved it.

* * * * * *

Lance was gorgeous. He had this way about him: He always looked clean, even after traveling all day. His go-to haircut with the side part had grown out slightly, but he still looked good to Journey. His skin was the color of caramel, and his lips protruded ever so slightly. His teeth were immaculate. He looked like a male model without the attitude.

The smell of Journey's favorite Versace men's cologne floated out to her, and she immediately began smiling.

Lance was on his phone and had not noticed Journey peering at him. She ran over to show him some love and put on a good act without letting him know what she had just gone through. Journey also needed some affection; the loss completely broke her. He kissed the top of her head and pulled her in close.

"Ooh, you smell good," Lance said, smelling Journey's hair.

I will never get tired of hearing that.

Although Journey couldn't give herself to him as he had expected, they still had a good night filled with kisses and cuddles.

She woke up the following day to a note on her bedside table that read: "Hey, my love, you looked so peaceful. I didn't want to wake you. I made reservations at Levor on Fifth Avenue for eight tonight. I want to talk to you about something. Love Lance :)."

Her feet met the floor quickly, and she ran to the bathroom and began cheesing a giddy smile in the mirror. Lance and Journey had been together for four years, and she was sure that he was about to propose! She could not shake her excitement! Journey believed that she and Lance were soulmates.

Originally from Brooklyn, they met at Yale when Journey was in law school, and Lance was pursuing his MBA. Although they were both in relationships, they became good friends. Journey was not someone who would cheat on their partner, so she kept it innocent and respectful. And once they both graduated, they lost touch.

It wasn't until a year later that Journey and Lance ran into each other at a comedy club in New York City. They were both single, and they saw each other in a different light. Lance told Journey that he knew she was the woman he had envisioned as his wife from the moment he met her, which caught Journey by surprise.

Lance loved everything about Journey. He loved how her black curls lay perfectly on her collarbone, and he loved her tan skin with its red undertones. To him, she stood at a perfect height of five feet three with a slim body frame. Journey had delicate, innocent eyes that Lance admired. Most of all, he respected the values and morals Journey upheld. He felt she was a woman of integrity, which made her an extremely rare find.

From that day on, they talked daily and eventually moved in together a year later. Journey believed in things working out for her, and reconnecting with Lance felt like destiny.

Oh my gosh, okay, I have to get my hair done, get a pedicure, manicure, everything!

* * * * * *

Journey called her best friend, Avery, to have some company. "Hey, Journ. Wassup?"

"Avery! Come over!"

"What has got you so excited this afternoon?" Avery asked through an innocent laugh.

"I'll tell you when you get here; just come!"

"Give me an hour; I'm just wrapping up with a client."

"OK, see ya!" said Journey.

When Avery arrived, Journey was too excited about dinner to tell her about the miscarriage. Avery was the only person that Journey had told about being pregnant. She didn't want to get any of her family's hopes up again. Journey would tell her about the miscarriage another time when the time felt right.

When Avery entered the door to Journey's apartment, Journey immediately shrieked, "Avery, I think it's time! I think Lance is going to propose!"

"No way! How do you know?" Avery asked, with a big grin cascading over her pearly whites.

Journey snatched the note from the table and pushed it into Avery's face.

Avery read it, looked at Journey, and said, "Oh my goodness, Journ! I hope he does propose. It is about time!"

Filled with excitement, Journ said, "Sooo? Are you coming with me to get my nails done or what?!"

Avery pretended to think about it, but then responded quickly, "Of course! Let's go!" while giving Journey a high five.

When they arrived at the nail salon, Journey and Avery looked at nail colors before the nail technician called Journey over. Journ's amazing nail lady, Lauren, waved to her, indicating she was ready.

On her way to Lauren's nail station with Avery, Journey accidentally bumped into a young lady, and all her belongings fell to the floor.

"Oh my goodness, I'm so sorry!" Journey whispered apologetically.

The young lady looked up at Journey, and Journey thought she looked familiar.

"No . . . no, don't worry about it," the young lady stammered.

"Lisa?!"

With bright eyes and a huge smile, Lisa responded, "Journey? Oh my goodness, how have you been? It's been forever!"

Once Journey finished helping Lisa pick up her scattered belongings from the floor, they stood up and were face to face.

"Aww, you're pregnant. You look amazing!" Journey exclaimed.

"Thank you, Journey; I am over the moon!"

With sincere eyes and joy, Journey shouted, "Well, congratulations! It was nice seeing you. I should get to my nail lady now," she said in a rush but with a smile and a laugh.

"Yes! It was nice seeing you, too; I will invite you to the baby shower!" Lisa called out as Journey was a few feet away.

"Can't wait!" Journ waved back at her.

Lauren took her time with Journey's nails, and they looked stunning. She wore a funny bunny color on her nails and white on her toes—the usual. Avery was just there for support like she always was.

As they were leaving the nail salon, Avery asked, "Who was that lady at the nail salon?"

"Oh, that was Lisa; she was a legal assistant at the firm I worked for right after I graduated from Yale—the one downtown. It was nice to see her," Journ said remembering their time at the law firm.

"Nice . . . nice. So what are you going to wear tonight?" Avery asked excitedly.

Through clenched hands and a big smile, Journey eagerly said, "I have the perfect outfit."

When Journey headed into the restaurant, she didn't bother telling the hostess her name because Lance was there to escort her to their table.

He smelled like her favorite cologne—Versace.

He wore a light blue button-up with no tie and tailored black slacks, and Journey wore a black satin gown that hugged her body in all the right places.

* * * * * *

As they walked to the table, his shoes made a "clack, clack" sound, and his hand rested comfortably over Journey's waist. His green eyes shimmered underneath the recessed lighting, and he had a fresh haircut with the usual side part, just like she liked.

She had never been to Levor's before, but she found it quite charming. It had the perfect dimmed lighting and red and black velvet curtains with gold and black trimming. It was not an ordinary restaurant—it specialized in French-inspired cuisine. The room smelled of sweet rolls and lobster bisque.

They ordered the best wine and talked for what seemed like hours. Journey barely had a chance to eat her pan-seared calamari. She asked for a to-go plate, and Lance requested the check.

"Hey, Journ, I want to tell you something."

"Yes?" She said with great anticipation. She sat up straight in the booth they were in.

Yes, it's finally happening, she thought.

"Um, I don't know how to tell you this," Lance said nervously.

"It's OK, babe; you can just say it," Journey said noticing Lance's nervousness.

"I haven't been honest with you," Lance said as he swallowed hard.

Uh oh. Journey took a big gulp of her wine. She was not expecting those words.

"I have a baby on the way with someone from my job. She has been working at the consulting firm for a while now," Lance said as he lowered his head with a look of shame.

Journey sat quietly for a moment. She tried to gather her thoughts as she silently debated whether she should be calm or jump over the table and strangle him.

"But I want to be with you. It was a mistake, and I have been feeling guilty these last few months since she told me she was pregnant," Lance continued to confess.

This man has known this for months?!

"Who is the woman?" she asked, trying to whisper calmly.

"It doesn't matter, Journ. Can we please work this out?"

"Who is she, Lance?" Journey asked firmly.

"Lisa, she helps some of the lawyers at the consulting firm from time to time. I know she used to work in your old office. But you have to believe me; this wasn't a planned decision, and it only happened once! I love you!"

This day could not get any worse.

* * * * *

Journey excused herself from the table to use the restroom. She needed some space from all the bullets she was catching from the words Lance was throwing.

The swinging bathroom doors were a burgundy red. Journey placed her hands on the door and pushed.

As soon as she entered, she ran into the bathroom stall and vomited; the night had made her physically ill.

She sat on the toilet, stared into space, and wondered when it went wrong.

Was it me? Did I do something to push him away? No, no, Lance's decisions were his and his alone. Do not blame yourself for this.

* * * * * *

Journey's feet were planted on both sides of the toilet. She felt an object beside her left heel. It was a small book with a leather cover. Curiosity got the best of her, and she picked up the book and opened it. It was a pocket-sized Bible filled with writing on little sticky notes.

This Bible obviously has an owner. What a weird place to leave it behind.

She opened the Bible to one of the sticky note pages. The sticky note was attached to 2 Timothy, chapter one verse seven, which was highlighted: *"For God gave us a spirit not of fear but of power and love and self-control."*

So, rather than returning to the table and giving Lance a piece of her mind, she calmed herself down in the bathroom and left with her head held high.

After a quick look in the vanity mirror, sprinkled with yellow lighting, she was ready to leave the lavender-scented, cream-tiled bathroom.

* * * * * *

Lance sat still, looking nervous. She could tell that he didn't know what to expect.

He had watched Journey grow over the past few years. She used to have extreme anger problems, but with the help of a therapist and anger management specialist, she was able to get a handle on it.

Though she would never touch him, she wanted to. And she believed he had feared that as well.

"Well," Journey spat out, "I think you should move out. I don't think the penthouse could fit us all . . . baby mama and all."

Ooo, I'm petty.

"But . . . but . . . I was hoping we could work through this. I really do love you, Journ," Lance mumbled.

Then why did you cheat? I don't get it when men say that.

Journey grabbed her purse and coat and headed for the restaurant's exit door. She left and didn't look back.

Although it would have been a good idea, Journey didn't consider the freezing temperatures outside or the fact that she had taken an Uber to the restaurant.

During the winter season, New York was not for the weak, but that did not stop Journey from leaving.

"Siri, call Avery," she said into her Apple watch while placing her AirPods in her ears.

She felt a cold hand on her shoulder. When she turned, she saw Lance's face staring blankly at her.

I never noticed how green his eyes are when he is sad. The scar under his eye is a little more noticeable now too.

Journ could feel his pain, but she was in more pain than he could begin to imagine. They stood face to face for seconds before Journey simply said, "I have to choose me. Goodbye, Lance," as she turned away from him.

She could feel the coldness of his absence as she continued to walk away. Her timing was perfect because just then, Avery answered her phone.

"Hey, girl! Did he propose? Tell me everything!" Avery said excitedly.

With tight lips, Journey whispered, "No. Hot chocolate at your house?"

"Oh no, Journ. What happened? You haven't drunk dairy since college. It must be bad. Come over."

"I'm already here. Please open up."

Avery conveniently lived two blocks from the restaurant. Because she was a successful real estate agent, she could afford to live in Manhattan.

When Avery opened the door, she saw that Journey's eyes were bloodshot red and droopy.

"Journ," Avery said sympathetically as a tear almost fell from her eyes. But she knew she had to keep it together for Journey. Journey did not look like herself. Avery urged her to come in out of the cold.

As usual, Journey was very put together. Her nails were painted a simple color; her hair was always perfectly done, whether pinned up into a bun or gracefully curly. Journey's eyebrows always looked spectacular. She had clear skin and no blemishes. Below her bottom lip was a perfectly placed beauty mark. She was beautiful.

But what Avery saw beneath the surface was not in the least bit beautiful. Journey was broken, and from the looks of it, nothing could mend her. As Avery opened the door, Journey ran into her arms and sobbed. Journey's legs became noodles, and she lost feeling in them. She dropped like a domino.

Avery had never seen her like that. She decided to call Journey's older sister Nya.

"Hey . . . uhm . . . Ny? Can you come over? It's an emergency; it's Journey."

"Wha . . . what happened? Is she OK?" Nya asked in a panicked voice.

"Yeah, she is physically fine, but she needs us," Avery pleaded.

"OK, I'll have Rob close the restaurant, and I'm on my way," Nya said haltingly as if struggling to breathe. "I'm running to my car now."

Journey was feeling very vulnerable and knew Avery would understand why she was so hurt by what happened with Lance. At that time, no one knew about her first miscarriage except Lance, Avery, and Journey.

When Nya arrived, Journey's eyes lit up with relief and joy.

Next to Avery, Nya was one of the people closest to Journey. She knew things about Journey that Journey didn't even know.

After about fifteen minutes of crying, Journey mustered enough energy to tell Avery and Nya what had happened.

Although Journey was a mess, she was intentional about what came out of her mouth.

"As you know, Avery . . . when Lance asked me to dinner at such an exclusive restaurant, I was sure that he would propose tonight, and I am rarely wrong. My gut told me . . . ," Journey said through sobs.

Avery and Nya stood there waiting for Journey to continue.

"Well, he did not propose; he gave me another gift I was not expecting."

CHAPTER 1

Avery's and Nya's faces were filled with confusion. They asked in unison, "So, why are you crying?"

Journey continued through muffled sobs; "Lance gave me the gift of honesty. He told me that he got Lisa pregnant."

"That lady from the nail salon!?" screamed Avery.

"Wait . . . Lisa . . . who? Lisa from the firm?!" Nya chimed in, looking between Avery and Journey.

"Yes," said Journey.

If Avery and Nya had known what had happened to Journey the night before, they would have felt the depth of pain Journey had experienced. Not only had she learned that Lance was having a baby with someone else, but she had also lost her baby, which she had to flush down the toilet in a tragic miscarriage. In addition to losing her baby, she had lost the father to another woman within a twenty-four-hour window.

Avery was aware of the first miscarriage, but Nya was not. And the only reason Avery knew was because she happened to be with Journey when it happened. Had Avery not been there, Journey would have taken that to the grave.

CHAPTER 2

Three weeks later

"Hey, baby!" Journey's mom, Luna, said excitedly in her soft southern accent as she wrapped her arms around Journey fully embracing her.

Journey had just arrived at her mom's house for the yearly Christmas party, which Journey loved. She loved almost everything about Christmas and spending time with her family. Sometimes, she dreaded going if that meant she had to see her extended family—uncles, aunts, and cousins. Her family was cool, but as she got older, she started to see right through their devious ways. Growing up, she thought she could trust everyone who was family. But soon, she realized that was not the case. She had to learn the hard way.

"Hi, Ma!" Journey said as she was suffocated by the food in her arms and her mom's bosom. "Ma, can I get in the house first? Geesh," she snickered. "Where's Dad?" Journey asked as she walked into her parents' cozy two-story colonial home.

"Oh, he's still getting ready upstairs; you know him," Mama Luna replied, waving carelessly toward upstairs.

"Aha, getting ready for what? To sit on the couch and eat?" asked Journey, laughing.

Journey placed the food on the dining room table, but not before her brother Zelle snuck a peek inside the aluminum foil-covered pan and asked, "You brought the mac and cheese, right? I don't want Mom's milky mac."

"Of course! I wouldn't do that to y'all," Journey said playfully.

Zelle was the oldest sibling, and he was the only boy. Throughout his thirty-two years, he had been through a lot. As a teenager, Zelle often got in trouble; even with his parents' steadfast love and guidance, he would never listen. Zelle eventually got involved with drugs and gangs at the age of fifteen. Their mom was so disappointed because all her children were born and raised in a Christian home where they went to church every Sunday and Bible study every Tuesday. So when Mama Luna found out Zelle was getting into trouble in the streets, she was heartbroken and turned to praying diligently for her son.

When Zelle turned eighteen, he was out with friends when a rival gang approached him and his crew. As a result, Zelle was stabbed multiple times and almost lost his life. He lost so much blood that the doctors didn't know whether he was going to live. After a week in the hospital with tubes coming out of his body, Zelle was finally able to walk. That stabbing left him with a five-inch laceration from the top of his neck down to his shoulder blade.

Fortunately, Zelle gave his life to God after that. At twenty-three, he married an amazing woman, and they had a son two years later. Zelle and his wife Martha are still going strong, and their son Blaze is indeed a blessing. Ever since Zelle turned his life around, he has been happy. In addition to owning a successful mechanic shop, Zelle is heavily involved in his church, and he has written songs for the local church choir, which gives him a deep sense of purpose.

Journey and Zelle caught up with each other in the dining room and discussed how life was going for them. Zelle cracked a couple of jokes, and Journey couldn't stop laughing. They had a tight bond, and Journey was so thankful to have Zelle as a best friend and a sibling.

Then Journey heard the front door open, and she caught a glimpse of Uncle Ernie and Cousin Pamela, out of the corner of her eye. Journey's heart sank.

She always felt weird and uncomfortable around Uncle Ernie but could never pinpoint why. He was a five-foot-five, beer-belly type of guy with pale brown skin, but he always looked like he was jaundiced or sick. Everyone loved him except Journey, and everyone knew it. It was strange because Uncle Ernie was her dad's brother, but the two of them had nothing in common.

As for his daughter Pamela, she was a bona fide hater. She always had something negative to say, and her way of saying things was a bit much for Journey, but Journey's sister Nya never invalidated those feelings; she was very supportive and understanding of them.

"Wassup, cousin!" Pamela shouted, but Journey knew that excitement was aimed at Zelle, not her.

While going in for a hug, Zelle said with a big smile, "Hey, Pam! What's going on? God bless!"

Pamela shot Journey a look. "Hi, Journey."

"Hey," Journey mumbled distractedly.

CHAPTER 2

Pam and Journey hugged the most awkward side hug.

Uncle Ernie gave Zelle a handshake and snuck a quick peck on Journey's cheek.

Journey quivered, but it wasn't noticeable to anyone except Nya, who was across the room witnessing the whole interaction.

Nya and Journey had an understanding. Their relationship as sisters was solid. Surprisingly, they never argued; at most, they had respectful disagreements at times. Since Nya was Journey's older sister, she made it her life's mission to protect Journey. Considering Nya knew Journey felt weird around Uncle Ernie and Cousin Pam, she always watched the interactions between Journey and them.

"Hey, Princess!" Journey turned around to see her dad descending the staircase from upstairs to enter the living room.

The house was Journey's childhood home, and even after thirty years, it was well-kept and immaculate. Journey's mom was an avid cleaner and did not play about Saturday morning deep cleanings, while praise and worship music could be heard throughout the house.

"Hi, Dad," said Journey as she hugged and kissed him on the cheek. Romero Sands was Journey's favorite parent. The bond she and her dad built was out of this world. Although Journey and her mother were close, being the youngest meant one parent would spoil Journey, and that parent was not Mama Luna.

Journey's dad was an amazing husband and father. Thanks to her dad, all the kids had traveled across the globe and had the time of their lives during their childhood years. He treated his wife like a queen, which set the tone for the children's perspective on love. That is probably why none of the siblings ever dated anyone they didn't think they would spend the rest of their lives with.

While Mama Luna was more of a disciplinarian, she made sure none of her kids quit anything they signed up for. She ensured they all knew how to clean well, and most of all, she taught them the importance of keeping their word, even as she showed them tons of love. But Journey's dad was the fun, lenient parent. There had to be balance.

Everyone was starving and ready to eat Christmas dinner. The food smelled spectacular, and they all felt it was time to fill their bellies. Everyone was there . . . except for Granny.

Granny was Mama Luna's mom and the sweetest person you could ever meet. She was from Welch, West Virginia, and brought her southern hospitality to New York, where they all lived. Granny was hands-down the best cook in the family, and her love for God made her comfortable to be around because no one ever felt judged by her. Everyone in the family had the utmost respect for her.

"Ma! I'm hungry," Zelle screamed from the living room into the kitchen.

"I know, I know, but we have to wait for Granny. No one is eating until she comes," Mama Luna hollered back.

While Dad, Uncle Ernie, and Zelle waited for Granny to arrive, they decided to watch Christmas Day football.

Nya was aware that Journey was on edge because of everything that had happened over the last few weeks. When Pamela came over to bother Journey with some meaningless drama, Nya could tell Journey did not have the patience for it.

"Have you gained weight? Where's your boyfriend? I suppose he thinks he's too good to come around for the holidays," Pamela said belligerently.

Journey showed restraint and stayed quiet. But Pamela kept talking.

"He dumped you, didn't he? Guess little Miss Perfect isn't so perfect after all."

Nya could see the smoke coming from Journey's head when she said, "Pamela, all you do is judge us! But have you taken a second to look in the mirror? Girl, you've been through more boyfriends this past year than I have underwear. You're toxic!" Journey screamed, which shook the whole atmosphere.

Mama Luna and Dad were shocked. Zelle looked confused, and Nya was ready to escort Journey out, but Journey was on a rampage.

Before Pamela could respond, Uncle Ernie shouted, "Don't talk to my daughter like that! Are you out of your mind?! You always thought you were better than Pam, but you're not! You can't even have children!" Uncle Ernie's words pierced everyone's ears.

Journey's mouth began to quiver. It was a random comment, but it hit its mark. How did he know Journey was struggling to have a child? She pushed through the tears and calmly said, "No disrespect, Uncle Ernie, but no one was talking to you. I am sick and tired of dealing with y'all and your drama. I am done pretending to like y'all; I don't!"

The anger on Uncle Ernie's and Pamela's faces was evident to everyone in the house. With a rush of movement, Uncle Ernie got up frantically and shouted, "We are leaving! Get your things, Pam!"

Journey ran to the bathroom almost immediately to cool off. She never liked getting angry to that point because it was so powerful that it took over her consciousness, and she would often black out.

While calming herself down in the bathroom, she heard a knock on the door and Nya's voice.

"Hey, Journ, may I come in?"

Journey let Nya in, and she noticed that Nya was crying and had a guilty look on her face.

"Journey . . . ," Nya whimpered.

Before Nya could finish, another knock at the door interrupted them; it was their dad.

"Hey, Princess, are you OK?"

"I'm sorry, Dad, I just can't keep pretending anymore. Life is too short, and I shouldn't have to deal with this," Journ said as she splashed water on her face. "I don't care if they are family. Family hurts you the most!"

"Princess, I know you are hurting. I can see it on your face. But let's have a good rest of Christmas; this day is very special to you."

Journey was able to calm herself down and prepare to eat. When Journey, Nya, and Dad left the bathroom, a weight was lifted from Journey. However, Journ hadn't figured out why Nya was crying; she was never one to cry.

Finally, Journey heard, "Hi y'all. How's my grandbabies?" Granny excitedly greeted everyone as she walked through the tall glazed burgundy front door.

Granny always had a way of uplifting her family. Her presence helped to bring peace to a disaster. If her presence did not do enough, her famous banana pudding would.

"Granny!" Journey screamed and ran to hug her.

"Oh, baby, what's the matter?" Granny asked.

"I just missed you, Granny; that's all."

"Mm, Grandmama knows her grandbabies," Granny said with an accusatory look.

After everyone ate until their bellies were full, they settled down. Journey was ready to head home because she was exhausted. She hadn't eaten much, and she experienced some stomach pain that intensified after the argument with Pam and Uncle Ernie.

Journey was unsure whether it was a good or bad thing that no one brought up what had happened earlier. Part of her felt like the rest of the family had her back, and there was nothing to say. But then another part of her believed that maybe the rest of her family didn't find the situation as severe as she did.

Zelle made his way over to Journey; she was sitting on the window seat in the living room, looking out at the snow falling to the ground.

"So, Sis, when am I going to see you at church?" Zelle asked softly.

Journey smiled a short and innocent smile and said, "Soon, Bro, I promise. I just have a lot of stuff going on right now."

"Give it to God; he knows all about it."

Journey didn't want to hear that at the moment. She struggled to understand what God was doing with her life.

Mama Luna walked over and chimed in, "I know that's right!"

They all laughed a contagious laugh. It was nice.

Before Granny left, she whispered something to Journey. But she couldn't make out the words. It sounded like Granny said, "I know," and grinned at Journey.

Journey was perplexed because she had no idea what Granny said, but she was too tired to question her.

"Bye, Granny . . . love you."

Journey prepared to leave shortly after Granny left. She began saying her goodbyes to everyone and then headed toward the front door and out to her SUV, which was parked in her parents' driveway.

Once she reached her car, she felt someone behind her. It was Nya. Journey could see the guilt in her eyes again, but this time, it appeared that there was hurt in her eyes as well.

Tears fell down Nya's face as she uttered, "Uncle Ernie, he . . . he did something to you when you were younger."

What?

CHAPTER 3

"Why don't I remember?" asked Journey blankly. "When everything happened, you were so angry. You were so young."

When Nya placed that load on Journey, they decided that they needed to talk it out and process everything that night.

Surprisingly, Journey did not cry; she just took it all in. She was numb to the news Nya shared.

"Let's go to the riverbank, around the corner where we used to go to as kids," Nya suggested. "I'll text Zelle to let him know that I left with you; I don't want anyone to worry."

"Yeah, that's a good idea," Journey said.

When Nya and Journey arrived at the riverbank, it was too cold to get out of the car, so they just sat and talked. She and Nya talked for hours; Journey had so many questions. It was around midnight before Nya and Journey realized how late it was. Journey dropped Nya back at their parents' house and decided to head home.

"Text me when you get home, Journ. I might just crash here at Mom and Dad's house. I love you."

Journey nodded and said, "OK. Love you too."

When Journey got home, she immediately ran to the bathroom, purse still in hand. She began to vomit profusely. That night had been incredibly overwhelming and nauseating for Journey. It also didn't help that Journey barely ate anything at dinner.

Journey was so physically weak that she was barely able to wipe her mouth and walk to her room, which was next door. She fell asleep on the storage bench at the foot of her bed.

Had she not been so utterly exhausted, it would have been difficult for Journey to sleep in the bed she and Lance once shared.

* * * * * *

Journey was awakened by the daylight beaming through her curtains and her cell phone buzzing. Disoriented, Journey searched for her phone and answered it.

"Hello?" Journey said while rubbing her eyes.

"I've been trying to reach you, Journey!" screamed Avery. "Guess who I saw at the mall?"

"Who?" Journey asked while still trying to collect herself.

"Lance and his little girlfriend, Lilly?"

"Aha . . . , Lisa?" Journey asked while getting out of bed.

"Yes, her! It turns out they have been dating for over a year. She didn't even know y'all dated!"

"There's no way!" Journey said with a little attitude.

"Nah, Journ, she didn't. But I didn't think it was my place to say anything. She just mentioned that they had been together; she was oblivious. The look on Lance's face was enough satisfaction for me," Avery said, chuckling.

"Well, let me call you later, Avery. I have to get myself together."

"OK, call me later! Don't forget."

"Bye, Avery."

Journey had two missed calls from Nya and missed texts from her parents.

After what Nya had told Journey the night before, Journey wasn't in the mood to talk to her family. She was too hurt.

She felt that the only person who understood the complexity of the situation was Nya. She knew Nya had kept the secret to protect her, but Journey wasn't sure why her parents never disclosed the secret.

Journey cleaned when she was stressed or overwhelmed. So she decided to deep-clean her apartment while she returned Nya's calls and talked to her.

"How could Mom and Dad let him around us after what he did?"

"It took a very long time. You didn't see how it ate at Dad for years. He wanted to kill Uncle Ernie. They had a huge falling out that lasted years. When Dad first found out, he beat Uncle Ernie badly. But I think Mom and Dad learned to forgive. They prayed and prayed, and eventually, they came around to having Uncle Ernie around for family events. He did things to me, too, Journ. I took that on, so you didn't have to be the victim. I hurt for a very long time. I was depressed for years and turned to drinking just to mask the hurt. But enough was enough. God and therapy helped me. Being raped by your one and only uncle messes with your mind."

"How old were we?" Journey asked through tears.

"You were ten, and I was thirteen.

"What he did was unforgivable!" Journey said, enraged.

"Mom and Dad also thought you suppressed the memory and that we never needed to talk about it. No parent is prepared to talk about something like that. To this day, I still cannot let him hug me. I quiver at his touch, and I don't think that will ever change."

"I can't even look at Mom and Dad now."

"This is a lot. No one is expecting you to come back from this immediately. Take your time to process this and figure out what you want to do next."

"Did you tell Mom and Dad that you told me everything?" Journey asked.

"I gave them a heads-up just in case you wanted to talk with them. Do you want to talk with them about this?" Nya inquired.

"Not now. I don't know if I will ever be ready for that conversation."

"Well, take your time. I will come over later and bring you dinner or something."

"OK, but not too late. I have to go back to work tomorrow."

"Oh, right. Okay. See you later, Journ."

While Journey was cleaning the house, she decided to clean out her purse. When she dumped everything out, she heard a "thump" on the floor; it was the annotated Bible from the restaurant.

How did that get in there? I do not remember taking it.

Journey opened the Bible. She saw the same Scripture she read at the restaurant that gave her the strength to keep going: 2 Timothy 1:7.

Journey took her phone out to text Zelle.

Journey: "Hey, Bro."

Zelle: "Hey, Sis. Wassup? "

Journey: "What time is the service on Sunday?"

Zelle: "Service is at eleven, but we have revival this week, and the visiting pastor is Pastor Phillips; I know you used to love his teaching. He will be speaking on Thursday and Friday."

Journey: "Cool, thanks. I will let you know what I decide."

Zelle: "I'm excited, Sis. I know you'll enjoy it. Come whenever. God bless."

Journey got an urge to listen to praise and worship music—like the music Mama Luna used to play when she cleaned.

The music helped. The Scripture helped. Journey felt powerful and strong.

This, too, shall pass.

Journey was watching *A Year Without a Santa Claus* when she heard the doorbell, it was Nya. She buzzed Nya in, and a few moments later, Nya was standing outside Journey's door holding Chinese food. Journey was so happy to see that food. She was starving.

"Ooh, my favorite. Start the movie over!" Nya exclaimed and raced toward the living room couch.

Journey restarted the movie in good spirits, and she and Nya spent that night watching Christmas movies and bonding.

Nya finally fell asleep, but Journey couldn't. All she could do was think of Uncle Ernie and how her parents knew and never said anything.

Since Journey had to return to work the following day, she tried to get some work done and mentally prepare to go into the office. It had been easy to hide from the world the past few weeks because this was the holiday season. But going into the office meant that Journey had to put on the best facade of her life. Although everyone at her job loved her, she did not hang out with them outside work. Journey liked to keep her private life private. It was much simpler that way. Journey stayed up that whole night while Nya slept the night away.

The sun exposed itself again, indicating it was time to start the day. Journey put on one of her favorite pantsuits and baby heels; she was ready to head to work. Journey said goodbye to a sleeping Nya and walked out the front door. Despite getting no sleep the night before, Journey felt excited to return to work. Being back at work felt normal to her. She liked having a routine, and it was the perfect distraction. Journey's work as a lawyer always kept her busy.

When she arrived at the office, she was greeted with smiles and waves. Her assistant, Carla, had ginger tea and a plain bagel with peanut butter waiting for her at her desk. Journey was ready to start the day.

As soon as Journey got settled in, there was a soft knock on her office door.

"Hi, Journey."

"Oh, hi, Joey. How's everything?"

Joey was Journey's coworker and Carla's husband. Journey liked Joey because they both started at the firm at the same time, and they were both ambitious. Journey often found herself in an awkward space because she knew that Carla sometimes flirted with her coworkers behind Joey's back, but Journey thought it best to mind her business. She thought that Joey could have done better. Carla wasn't as ambitious as he was, and Journey saw that this bothered Joey sometimes.

"Good, good. I wanted to pick your brain about some briefings I'm preparing. I know you are off next week, so I wanted to grab you before it was too late," Joey said with a smile.

"Sure, of course! Give me a few hours, and maybe we can discuss them over lunch." Journey offered.

"Sounds good. I will come get you around noon."

Journey flashed him a thumbs-up.

She got a lot of work done in a short period of time; that was how Journey was. Law came easy to her, and she never minded helping others around her. As a criminal defense attorney, she sympathized with her clients, which made her the best.

Mondays meant preparing for court for the week. She had an explicit schedule every week. She would only spend a couple of days a week in the office as she was in court the rest of the week. Journey hated the tediousness of having to continue cases because she felt her client's life was on the line and that pushing court dates out unnecessarily was not fair.

Noon came quickly, and Joey arrived to grab Journey for lunch. They ate lunch in the conference room while Joey reviewed several cases with Journey. One case caught Journey's attention.

"I have this young woman who is willingly pleading guilty to a crime even though the evidence doesn't prove she did it. She is accused of murdering her long-time boyfriend over a minor disagreement. He was found with multiple gunshot wounds to the back. I've seen many killers in my time as an attorney, and she is not a killer. How do I convince her not to plead guilty and let me fight for her?"

"This sounds like a fascinating case. What is the district attorney proposing?"

"Well, we are both stumped, but it seems like an easy win for the DA if we don't take it to trial. I will visit the defendant in jail on Wednesday to see if we can agree before her arraignment."

"Well, what evidence do they have that has you thinking it wasn't her?" Journey asked quizzically.

"There was no blood on her, and there was no gunshot residue beneath her fingernails. The gun was found on the scene, but there is no DNA on it. It is a strange case."

"Hmm, yeah, that does seem strange. Mind if I come with you on Wednesday? I won't go into the room with you; I will watch from behind the two-way mirror. I want to understand who she is and how she interacts with you. Maybe I can help you figure out what to do."

"Sounds good to me," Joey agreed.

For the rest of Journey's workday, she began reading more about the young woman Joey was telling her about: Lillyann Fisher. Journey read about Lillyann's life and looked through Joey's paperwork on the case. She was invested, so she was the last person in the office. Work felt like a breath of fresh air for Journey; she almost felt whole again.

But when Journey got home, she was faced with her reality and her trauma. The situation had been eating at her so much that she was not getting much sleep. The nightmares about Uncle Ernie, the sad reality of not becoming a mother, and breaking up with the love of her life overwhelmed her with a windmill of feelings.

As soon as Journey got home, she received a call from Avery.

"Come outside! I'm here to pick you up. I haven't heard from you. Let's go out."

Avery was Journey's best friend since childhood, but Journey felt she should keep family business in the family.

"Uh, I'm not really in the mood. I have a lot of stuff to get done for work. I'll catch up with you later," Journey said, distracted.

Avery felt hurt by that. No matter what Journey went through, she always made time to hang out with Avery. Avery wondered what was up with Journey, so she called Nya.

"Hello?" said Nya.

"Hey, Nya, it's Avery. I just pulled up to Journey's apartment. She seemed off and didn't want to come hang out, which isn't like her."

"Yeah, she's been through a lot. Just give her some time."

"I mean, I know the breakup was a lot. But it's been over a month, so I thought she would be getting better. The last time I saw her this down was when she had that miscarriage."

"Wait, what did you say? A miscarriage? Journey was pregnant? When was this?" Nya asked in disbelief.

"You didn't know? This was almost a year ago. So, wait, what did you think I was talking about? What has been going on?"

"I thought you were talking about everything that happened on Christmas."

"What happened during Christmas? Journey said everything went well," said Avery.

"I don't think it's my place to say. You're going to have to ask her."

"Nya, I told you something you didn't know. Now you should tell me what I don't know. I just want to know what's going on with her."

"I'd rather tell you in person. Meet me at Starbucks on Fifth Street in an hour, K?"

"Got it," said Avery confidently.

When Nya and Avery met, the air was thick. They both carried heavy secrets, making them feel as though they were betraying Journey's trust. But certain things were meant to be shared. Journey's trauma should not have to be something to hide.

Nya ordered a latte while Avery waited in anticipation.

Nya began, "Long story short, Journey was dealing with some things that had to do with our Uncle Ernie. On Christmas Day, Journey had a big argument with him, and then she later found out that Uncle Ernie sexually assaulted her when she was younger."

Avery's silence was loud. Her face turned pale, and tears began streaming from her eyes down to her mouth.

Nya took some deep breaths and added, "So, I'm sure all this is taking a toll on her. But one thing I know about my sister is that she will need her space for now, but when she is ready, she will reach out."

"But that's the thing, Nya, I don't think she will be ready. She's going to bury this too. I feel like she regrets telling me about the miscarriage because I know Journey doesn't like it when we show pity."

"I'm afraid you may be right. But I pray you aren't," Nya said hopefully.

CHAPTER 4

"I'm so nervous. I haven't been to church since maybe high school," Journey admitted.

Standing in Journey's living room, Zelle reassured her. "You'll be fine. Everyone will be happy to see you, especially God. That is all that matters," he said.

"I'm almost ready, just putting my shoes on," Journey yelled from her bedroom.

Journey had had a great and productive week at work, so she thought it best to end the week by going to Revival, as Zelle had suggested.

When Journey arrived at church, her old congregation members welcomed her with hugs and smiles. Zelle still went to the church he and his siblings had attended when they were young: Christ the King Church. They were Pentecostal, which Journey thought meant they were Christians who "shout" and "jump around."

During the service, Journey felt different. She felt lighter, both physically and emotionally. The atmosphere was intoxicating. When the choir began singing, Journey stood up and sang along. That put a smile on Zelle's face. Because Zelle was on fire for the Lord, he wanted everyone else to be, especially Journey.

Pastor Phillips delivered a wonderful sermon on the importance of forgiveness and how holding onto things could be detrimental. "If you don't forgive those who have wronged you, God will not forgive you. If God can be merciful to us after all we have done, why can't we show the same grace?" That stuck with Journey; she made a mental note to explore that notion more, maybe by praying and reading her Bible later that night.

When Pastor Phillips finished his sermon, he offered an altar call, an opportunity for those desiring prayer to come to the altar and be prayed for.

Journey decided to go up for prayer. When it was her turn, Pastor Phillips smiled at her. She had liked Pastor Phillips when she was growing up; he often referred to her as his "daughter in Christ." So, she felt comfortable letting him pray over her. He whispered something in her ear as he placed his hand over Journey's head and prayed over her. "God is pleased that you came to church today; He told me to tell you that He already worked it out; a miracle is coming. Praise Him in advance!" Journey immediately began weeping uncontrollably and fell into Pastor Phillips's arms. She eventually fell to the floor in total surrender, and she received her breakthrough. After the church service, Journey was at peace with everything and could share without feelings of anger seeping into her soul. She felt free.

As Zelle drove Journey home, she told him about everything that had been going on.

"I am so glad you encouraged me to go to church tonight, Zelle. It changed my life. When Pastor Phillips prophesied over me, I felt the presence of God and knew I could triumph over all my pain."

Until that night, Journey hadn't realized that she was burying her emotions and letting work distract her. She had led herself to believe she was okay and that she had gotten over everything she was dealing with, so much so that she hadn't spoken to either Nya or Avery for the past few days.

With a huge smile, Zelle said, "Despite hearing all this news, I am so happy you came out tonight. God has a plan for you, Journ."

Journey felt good going to work the next morning. It was Friday, her last day before she had a week off. When she got to work, Carla told Journey that Joey was waiting in her office.

With a big grin, Joey said, "Hey, Journ!"

Journey laughed and asked, "What has got you in such a good mood this morning?"

"After we debriefed about my meeting with Lillyann at the jail, I took your advice."

"OK, great! How did it go when you followed up with her yesterday?"

"She wants to fight! She plans on entering a not-guilty plea!"

"Oh my gosh, Joey! That's great; I am so happy for you," Journey said while hugging Joey. "I watched her as you were talking with her the other day, and I knew immediately she had the face of a woman who was grieving for her partner. Something else happened in that house the night he died, and I pray she helps put the real killer in jail!"

"I want you to be my co-counsel on this case," Joey blurted out.

"Oh wow, um . . . this is a surprise. I wasn't expecting that," Journey said.

"You're right . . . you're right; I think I got a little too excited. But I still want you to work this case with me if you are up to it."

"Let me think about it. I'll let you know what I decide," Journey replied.

"Great! Thanks again," he said as he left Journey's office.

Journey wanted to say yes immediately, but being impulsive never served her well. She knew this would be a massive case and that Lillyann's sister was paying big money to have Johnson & Associates represent her sister.

Journey stayed late once again. On her way out of the office, she passed Joey's office and heard raised voices. Journey backtracked to the fishbowl office and saw that Joey and Carla were arguing. Joey was sitting at his desk while Carla was standing over the desk facing him with her back toward the door. It looked like no one else was in the office, so luckily, no one else heard.

Journey approached Joey's office and knocked softly. She didn't care that they were arguing; she acted as if she did not hear it.

"Hey, Carla, I'm headed out. Direct any emergency calls to the secretary while I am away next week."

"Will do, Journey," Carla said without turning around.

Journey assumed she might have been crying.

"Oh, Joey, I would love to join you as co-counsel. When I come back, you can get me caught up, and we can start planning everything. See y'all!

"Bye, Journey!" Carla and Joey said in unison.

When Journey got home, she couldn't wait to have dinner and relax. She ordered Spanish food from down the street. When her order arrived, she ran to her apartment lobby to grab it.

After she got her food, she was heading up the stairs until she heard someone shout her name.

"Journey!"

It was a man's voice.

It was Lance.

Uh oh.

Journey continued to walk toward her apartment, knowing Lance would follow her. She didn't want to cause a scene in the lobby.

Once Journey unlocked her door, she opened it and motioned for Lance to walk in. Then she shut the door behind her.

"What's up, Lance?" Journey asked while taking her food out to eat. She was quite poised but also irritated that Lance had the nerve to show up. He was lucky that Journey happened to be in the lobby because she would never have willingly let him in.

"I miss you, Journ. I feel horrible," Lance said with sincere eyes.

"It's been weeks, and now you feel horrible?" Journ questioned.

"It has been rough these past few weeks."

Yeah, you look like it.

"Are you happy?" Journey asked.

"I mean, I'm happy that I'm going to be a father to a baby boy."

A baby boy?

He continued, "But I'm not happy with the person I'm having the kid with. I'd much rather have had a kid with you, Journ. I love you, and it will always be you. I don't want to be with Lisa. I want to be with you."

It would be tough for Journey to get back with Lance now that he had a kid on the way. She always promised never to date someone with a kid if she didn't have one.

All Journey could do was shed a tear. No words. She felt kind of sorry for him for a second until he spoke those words: "You have to understand how I felt. I loved you, and I wanted to marry you! When you lost the baby, I was hurt, and if I am being honest, I blamed you for the miscarriage."

"You blamed me?! I did nothing wrong," Journey said as tears continued to cascade down her face.

"I know . . . I know. I am not trying to upset you. I'm just sharing all I felt, which ultimately led to my transgressions."

Journey didn't know what to say. What does anyone say to that?

Journey wiped her tears and said calmly and emotionlessly, "Well, then, I guess you should know that I had a miscarriage the night you came home from Florida."

Lance began to weep and approached Journey with his arms outstretched. Journey allowed him to hug her, but she didn't return the favor; she stood still.

"I am so sorry, Journ; why didn't you tell me?"

"There was nothing you could do, Lance, and I didn't have the energy to relive that pain like I am now," admitted Journey.

Of course, Journey still loved Lance. It had only been a few weeks, and you don't fall out of love with someone that fast, even if that someone has hurt you.

Journey thought about asking Lance more about Lisa, but she didn't think that would help at all. But she couldn't help herself.

"So, how long were you and Lisa messing around?"

"I wouldn't say messing around. We only had sex once, and that was less than a year ago."

"Are you two together now? Avery told me about the run-in at the mall."

"No, no, no; we aren't together. I made it very clear that I will be in the baby's life, but I don't want to be in a relationship with her. That was a one-time thing," Lance continued.

"Avery told me that y'all have been messing for about a year," Journey said accusingly.

"Avery has a big mouth because that is not the case. When we ran into her at the mall, Lisa said that to Avery, and I was shocked that she straight-up lied. She knew about you and me when she and I had sex together. Lisa is trying to make herself seem like the innocent victim, but she is not."

"You really expect me to believe you? Why were you even at the mall together?" asked Journey.

"We were stopping by to create the list for the gift registry; that's it."

"Whatever, Lance. I honestly don't even care anymore," Journey said.

"I don't believe you," Lance said while grabbing Journey's arms and looking into her sad eyes.

"Lance, get off me," Journey said weakly.

Lance knew how to butter Journey up. He kissed her neck slightly and then moved to her lips. Journey tried to remain strong, but she couldn't. She gave into the seduction.

Lance carried Journey to the bedroom, and they made love underneath the star-gazing sky. Afterward, they just stared at each other. Journey began to cry; she felt so guilty and a little embarrassed. Lance wiped her tears away and suggested he leave, which only made Journey feel worse, but Lance didn't notice.

Lance put his clothes on and kissed Journey on the cheek. "I'll call you later, Journ."

Journey immediately fell ill. She ran to the bathroom and threw up. *Something has got to give.*

Journey was losing weight, and she didn't even notice. Ever since the Christmas party, she had been unable to keep food down. Afterward, Journey began to feel some pain in her stomach, similar to the pains she felt at the party, only sharper.

To her surprise, Lance hadn't left the apartment yet, and he ran into the bathroom when he heard Journey. He ran to her aid and helped her clean herself up.

"You don't look well, Journ. You should go to the hospital."

"I will be fine; just leave. I'm going to shower, which should help relieve some of this pain. Can you bring me a glass of water to take some Advil?"

Lance returned to the bathroom with a glass of water and Advil in hand. Journey was already in the shower, so Lance left everything on the bathroom sink. "I'm going to hang out until you're finished to make sure you are OK."

"Whatever," said Journey. She didn't have the time or the energy to kick Lance out. The stomach pains were growing more intense, and she kind of liked the company.

While Journey was in the shower, Lance decided to turn on the TV and watch basketball. Once he got comfortable, he heard a loud knock at the front door. He turned down the volume on the TV and raced toward the door.

It was Nya.

"What the hell are you doing here?" Nya questioned.

"I was here to talk to Journey," Lance explained.

"Haven't you done enough? She is hurting because of you!" said Nya as she pushed past Lance to get inside the apartment.

"I know . . . I know. I came to apologize. You know I love her, Nya; let me explain," Lance pleaded.

Nya walked around the apartment and said, "There's nothing to explain, Lance. You can go! Where is Journey?"

"She's in the shower; she wasn't feeling well—

A loud thud from the bathroom interrupted Nya and Lance's conversation.

"Journey!" Nya yelled.

Lance and Nya headed toward the shower only to find that Journey had fallen. She lay on the bathroom floor, not moving, and her eyes were closed.

Nya shook Journey and eventually got her to open her eyes.

"Journey, we have to get you to the hospital!" Nya said. "Make yourself useful, Lance, and grab Journey a towel and some clothes."

Lance carried Journey to Nya's car, and the three of them headed to the closest emergency room, forty-five minutes away. When Journey wasn't dozing off, she was groaning in agony. Lance and Nya grew worried the longer they were in the car. This wasn't the time for arguing; they had to figure out what was wrong with Journey.

CHAPTER 5

The wait was not long when Lance, Nya, and Journey finally arrived at the emergency room.

The doctors ran tests and then prescribed painkillers, but they only made the pain worse. Finally, a doctor came into the room where Journey, Lance, and Nya were and asked Journey a few questions.

"When did the pain start?"

"I have been experiencing pain for the last few weeks, but this time it is more intense."

"Is there anything that triggers these pains?" the doctor asked.

"Hmm, certain foods, and sometimes I even throw it up," Journey confessed.

The doctor applied pressure to Journey's stomach and pelvis. "Does it hurt when I do this?"

Journey nodded her head and groaned.

"OK, it may be kidney stones or possibly appendicitis. I will have my nurse do an ultrasound to see what may be causing these symptoms."

The nurse applied ultrasound gel to Journey's abdomen and lower stomach area and began moving the wand around Journey's stomach. "I see a lot of fluid in your stomach," she said. The nurse continued to roll the wand around and then stopped. "The doctor will be back shortly to review possible diagnoses for you."

Shortly after, the doctor returned to the room and reviewed Journey's symptoms to ensure he addressed all of Journey's concerns.

"Your blood levels are normal, and you don't have any inflammation. What is concerning is that your HCG levels are high. The nurse believes you to be pregnant. She saw a fetus during the ultrasound."

"Wait . . . what did you say?" Journey asked, confused and in a state of disbelief.

"Yes, Ms. Sands, it looks like you are about ten weeks pregnant."

Journey laughed. "I'm sorry, doctor, you must have the wrong test results. I had a miscarriage about six weeks ago. I saw the still fetus. There's no way, and I certainly haven't had sex since."

Tonight doesn't count.

Lance was just as confused but also interested because he had no idea what was happening. He looked back and forth from the doctor to Journey as they spoke.

"No, Ms. Sands, you are, in fact, pregnant. I've only heard of a similar case to this one time before. Most likely, you were pregnant with twins and lost one; it is called the vanishing twin syndrome. It is a condition in which the mother miscarries one twin while the other survives. All the symptoms you are experiencing are consistent with pregnancy. That explains why you are feeling sensitive to certain foods, throwing up, and experiencing intense stomach pain."

"But wait, I have been bleeding every month. Is that normal?"

"Have you been under a lot of stress lately?"

Nya intervened. "Yes, she has!"

"Stress could be the cause of your spotting and possibly even your pain. When you're pregnant, you aren't supposed to take certain painkillers, which is why the pain has gotten worse."

Journey didn't know whether to cry happy tears or sad tears.

"We should get you caught up on prenatal care," the doctor suggested. The doctor prescribed medicine that would help Journey with her nausea and stomach pains.

Lance was sitting in the corner of the room with his face in his hands. Journey couldn't tell if he was excited or if he felt torn.

But Journey was too stunned to speak.

As they drove back to Journey's apartment, they were silent. Journey was in shock, and Lance and Nya were waiting for Journey to say something.

"What should I do, Ny?" Journey asked blankly.

"What do you mean? You have always wanted to be a mother."

Lance interjected eagerly, "You're going to keep it, right?"

Journey slowly turned to face Lance, who was sitting in the back seat. "Yes, I want to keep it, but what should we do?"

Although Journey wanted to be a mother, she also wanted to be a wife. But she and Lance were no longer together, and he was expecting a child with someone else, so Journey didn't know how to feel about that. She didn't want to share Lance with another woman. She was still extremely angry with Lance but hurt took over with this news.

Journey believed Lance did what he did because he thought they could never have a child. But now that it was possible for her to have a baby, she couldn't help but envision her life with Lance again. But she knew she couldn't relay that to Lance; she had to stand on her word.

"I will take care of my responsibility as the father of that child."

"Who said you were the father?" Journey barked.

OK, that was hurtful.

With that, Lance stayed quiet for the rest of the car ride. When they reached Journey's apartment, he didn't bother going upstairs or saying goodbye. He immediately transferred from Nya's car to his own and drove off.

Once Nya and Journey were inside her apartment, Nya said, "That was cold, Journey. He did not deserve that."

"What about me? Think of all he did! Are you saying that he just gets a pass, and I must deal with it?"

"That's not what I am saying, but after all we found out today, I don't think you should have said what you said. With the baby, we have to be a united front," Nya said kindly, holding Journey's shoulder.

"Maybe. But I always thought I would have someone to share a kid with," Journey stated.

"You will! You will still have Lance."

Journey rolled her eyes.

Nya continued, "Well, now you should take it slow at work and plan to take on less responsibility there."

"Oh snap . . . , work." Journey pressed her hands to her head. "I totally forgot I agreed to be Joey's co-counsel for a big case."

"Well, it looks like you will have to disagree," Nya said, laughing. As Nya walked backward toward the door, she said, "I have to get going. Call me if you need anything, and let me know when your next doctor's appointment is."

"Bye, Ny," Journey said as she closed her door.

Journey immediately called Zelle after Nya left to tell him everything that had occurred.

"Hello," Zelle answered. "Journ, are you there?" Zelle asked.

Journey couldn't stop crying, but she said, "I'm here."

"What's wrong?"

Journey took a moment before she answered, "Everything. I just found out I am pregnant."

"Congratulations, Journ! Why don't you sound excited? I thought this is what you wanted," Zelle said, confused.

"I did. I do. But this isn't how I expected my life to be when it happened," Journey said, feeling discouraged.

"This is a blessing from God; you better embrace it, or he will take it away. God's plans are not always our plans. Plus, you don't know whether you'll get back together with Lance or not."

What Zelle said left Journey feeling guilty for feeling the way she did, but she couldn't help but be enraged by how everything had turned out.

"I doubt it. I am so angry with Lance," Journey blurted.

"Don't let the devil use you. You had a breakthrough last night; don't let him steal your joy. You said you had forgiven Lance and that you were moving on. Why would you be angry with him?"

"I'm just so hurt. The love of my life went off and got another woman pregnant. Now I'm pregnant, and I don't know what to do or how to feel. I just feel rage. Why would God allow this to happen?"

"You know God doesn't make us do anything. He gives us free will, and Lance made that choice. But there's another player in this game: the devil. He stirs up trouble, but what he meant for your bad God meant for your good."

"You're right," Journey said in surrender.

"Just pray on it. Don't make any decisions yet. Just give it to God."

"Thanks, Zelle. I love you. Bye."

When Journey got off the phone, she decided to take Zelle's advice. She started looking for a Bible but realized she didn't have one. Then Journey remembered the Bible she had found at the restaurant weeks ago.

She looked at the kitchen table, where she last left it. As she sifted through all the unopened mail, she saw a blue envelope on top of the Bible. She opened it, and her jaw immediately dropped, and her mood went cold again. It was an invitation to Lance and Lisa's baby shower.

How long has this been sitting here? The baby shower is in two weeks.

Journey couldn't bring herself to read her Bible or pray. She sat in complete silence on her living room couch, staring at the wall. She had reached the point of total numbness. She felt nothing, less than nothing.

She eventually fell asleep but woke up to her phone ringing. It was Avery.

"Hello," said Journey.

"Well, hello, stranger! Where have you been? I have been trying to give you space, but I miss my best friend," Avery admitted.

Journey chuckled. "I miss you too. Feel free to come by. I know it's past midnight, but I'm not doing anything."

"I will be there shortly," said Avery happily.

When Avery arrived, Journey gave her the biggest hug. They hadn't seen each other in weeks, and it was nice for them to be reunited.

"What's going on!?" Journey said, looking at Avery and smiling.

"Nothing much. Work has been steady since there aren't any new listings right now. What's new with you?"

"Uhm, nothing new. I've just been wrapping up things at the office in time for my vacation next week. Oh, and I slept with Lance last night, well, a few hours ago, technically. Oh, and I also just found out I'm ten weeks pregnant," Journey said nonchalantly.

Avery spat out the water she was drinking. She was in total shock.

"What the hell, Journ?" Avery was speechless.

Journey laughed. "Yup, my life is an absolute mess. But anywho . . . are you planning to come with me to Lisa and Lance's baby shower next week?"

"Journey, . . . what? Why would you go after all that has happened? I don't think that is a good idea."

"Although I am unhappy with Lance, Lisa is still an old friend, and she invited me. I am going to at least show face."

After much hesitation, Avery agreed to go to the baby shower with Journey. Avery lightened the mood by talking about Journey's baby and her pregnancy.

"I'm going to be the godmother, right?" Avery asked rhetori-cally. "Because I already have so many ideas for the baby shower!"

That made Journey laugh. Avery always had a way of making Journey feel loved without doing anything but cracking a couple of jokes. Everyone knew not to ask Journey too many questions because when Journey was ready, if she ever was, they knew she would share then.

After many laughs and a couple of shrimp tacos that Avery had gotten delivered from DoorDash, they called it a night. Avery left well after three in the morning. As soon as Avery left, Journey dozed off on her bed without undressing or removing her contacts.

When Journey woke up the following day, she felt OK.

"Alexa, play Earnest Pugh radio." Journey got in the shower and washed the whole night off. She even mustered up enough energy to exfoliate and shave her body.

When she got out of the shower, she put on some comfy clothes and decided to make breakfast: a Spanish omelet with turkey bacon to go with a glass of orange juice. Journey grabbed her phone to turn off the music and check out her notifications; it was nine thirty. She had a few unread text messages from Avery and Lance:

Avery: "Hey, Journ, I made it home!"

Lance: "Journ, I would be lying if I told you what you said didn't hurt me. And I don't even know why I'm venting to you about this, but you just make me crazy, and I can't stop thinking about you and what you said. Can we talk? Face to face?"

Journey couldn't deceive herself. She felt slightly interested in Lance's proposal to meet up. Deep down, she wanted to see him, but she wasn't sure what to do, so she left his message marked as "seen." Instead, she decided to text Avery back.

Journey: "Hey, Avery, what do you have planned for today? Do you want to head to spin class?"

Avery: "I'm free! Are you sure you can still do spin class . . . since you are pregnant and all?"

Journey: "Girl, I'm pregnant, not dead, lol. See you there at eleven thirty."

I'm pregnant. Wow, that is the first time I have said that out loud. Ha, I'm really pregnant.

CHAPTER 6

Journey had a fantastic week off, but her vacation was coming to an end. It was the Friday before she had to go back to work the following Monday. On top of that, Journey needed to prepare for Lisa and Lance's baby shower the following Saturday.

Carla had called Journey earlier that morning to let her know about a new case that required Journey's attention. So, Journey quickly stopped at the firm to grab some urgent mail regarding the case. She figured she would stop by the firm and then go shopping for an outfit to wear to the baby shower and to find a gift.

When Journey arrived at the firm, Carla saw her as she passed the front desk.

"Hey, Journey!"

"Hey, Carla! Where did you put the mail?

"Oh, right; I left it on your desk," Carla responded.

"Great, thank you!"

Journey headed to her office to pick up her mail, and instead of rushing out, she sat down for a moment. She decided to open the correspondence and respond to a few emails, so she wouldn't feel quite so swamped on Monday.

Journey saw Joey walk past her door and turn around when he noticed she was in there.

"Hey, stranger. Back so soon?" Joey shouted cheerfully.

"Um, not yet. I just stopped by to grab my mail and get caught up on my email." Journey stopped typing on her computer and gave Joey her undivided attention because he had come into her office and sat down in the chair in front of her desk. Journey could tell Joey wanted to stay, so she asked, "What's been going on with you? How is everything?"

"I didn't have a chance to check in with you last week. But I know you heard Carla and me arguing, and I wanted to apologize."

"Apologize? For what?" Journey questioned.

"I didn't want you to feel like you were in the middle and would have to choose a side."

"Choose sides? I'm confused. Why would I have to do that?"

"Oh, I thought girls told each other everything. Carla didn't tell you?"

"Tell me what?" Journey asked slowly and with some caution.

"We are getting a divorce. I filed a couple of weeks ago."

"Oh, no! I didn't see that coming. Is that what the argument was about?" Journey asked sympathetically.

"Kind of. Carla tried to convince me to go to her family's party before we broke the news to them. I told her no. She started crying and pleading with me to at least think about it.

After I thought about it, I figured I owed it to her family. I like them, and I know they loved me for Carla."

"Why did you want a divorce? If you don't mind me asking."

"Honestly. I haven't been happy for years. We have always argued about the same things. I finally realized that she would never change."

Journey got up and closed her office door, so no one could hear their conversation.

Joey continued, "She doesn't want to have children. She's comfortable being an assistant for the rest of her life and never plans to own anything. She lacks ambition, which does not align with what I want. I want kids and may eventually want to own a firm and leave New York."

"Wow. I guess I have some news of my own to share. I'm eleven weeks pregnant."

As soon as Journey got her last word out, Joey hugged her and said, "Congratulations!"

"Thank you," Journey responded, not expecting Joey's reaction.

"But that means I can't help you represent Lillyann's case."

"Oh," Joey said, disappointed.

"I will certainly be around to help you behind the scenes. Still, I must lessen my load, considering my history of miscarriage. I don't want or need any added stress or responsibility right now. I hope you understand."

Joey said good-naturedly, "You are absolutely right. But I was looking forward to working with the famous Journey Sands."

"Sorry, but back to your situation. How are you feeling about all this?"

"No worries, that news was a worthy distraction. But to answer your question, I am OK. I feel like a weight has lifted off me. It was hard to go through with it because, of course, I love Carla, but it was because I love her that I had to let her go. I'm not good for her, and she is not good for me."

A week passed, and Journey still had not responded to Lance's heartfelt text message. This was partly because she didn't know what to say and partly because she had been relaxing and had forgotten to respond. She knew she would see him at the baby shower.

Journey pulled up to the hall where the baby shower was to be held. Before she got out of the car, she wrote her name on a card and packed it into the gift bag with the baby clothes and diapers she bought.

Journey called Avery to see where she was and found out that Avery was still at home getting ready. So Journey walked into the hall alone. She figured she would go in and see what the vibes were while waiting for Avery.

She immediately spotted Lisa and Lance greeting the guests as they walked in. Journey was very early, so only a few people other than family were there. She figured if she went early, she could leave early. Journey didn't like social gatherings enough to stay long.

Lisa stole a hug from Journey and exclaimed, "Hi, Journey! Thank you so much for coming!"

Journey was genuinely happy for Lisa. But it was hard to see her with Lance.

Lance greeted Journey as casually as possible, but they both shared a glance of discomfort and tension. By the look on Lance's face, he was surprised and confused to see Journey there.

After chatting with Lisa, Journey decided to take a seat. While walking to an available seat at one of the wonderfully decorated white tables, Journey heard, "Journey, is that you?"

To Journey's surprise, it was Carla, and she was with Joey.

Carla and Joey approached Journey with outstretched arms.

"Hey, Joey and Carla! What are you doing here?" Journey asked, shocked and confused.

"We could ask you the same thing," Carla said.

"I'm here to support an old friend, Lisa," Journey explained.

"No way! Lisa is Carla's sister," Joey said excitedly.

"You're kidding!" Journey said while awkwardly scratching her arm.

Joey and Carla looked happy for a moment.

Carla's smile turned into a frown, "Wait . . . Lance. He was your boyfriend. He looked familiar. I remember him dropping lunch to you a few times."

Joey chimed in, "That's right . . . that's why he looked so familiar."

Carla explained, "I told Lisa that he was your boyfriend. Such a shame the way y'all broke up."

"Wait, you know why we broke up?"

Carla said, "Lisa told me she was interested in someone at work, and I thought nothing of it. But when she found out she was pregnant and told me she had been seeing this man from work named Lance, I got angry with her. I told her that you two were dating, but she told me that you cheated on Lance and broke up about a year ago."

So Lisa did know . . .

Journey's face turned red, and she tried to calm her nerves before answering. "I never cheated on Lance. We just broke up almost two months ago."

"Something is not adding up. If you two broke up two months ago, why is Lisa saying they have been together for over a year?"

"Good question. Let's go ask her," Journey said with fire in her eyes.

As Journey went to confront Lisa and Lance, Avery walked in with a big smile on her face, and when Avery saw the rage in Journey's eyes, she ran to stand beside her.

Joey, Carla, Journey, and Avery were walking toward Lance and Lisa, who luckily were alone and away from the party.

Journey was very direct but smooth with her words. "Hey, Lisa, I think we should get to the bottom of all these allegations surrounding your relationship with Lance," Journey said pointedly. "Have you two been dating for a year?"

"You're just mad because I have him now. Little Miss Perfect didn't get the boy," Lisa started but was quickly interrupted by Lance.

"Lisa, stop," Lance said, staring into her eyes. Lance turned to Journey with sympathetic but firm eyes. "No, Journey, I told you. We weren't dating. We never dated. It was a drunken night."

"Don't lie, Lance, tell her what you told me. Tell her you wanted a family; that was the one thing she couldn't give you. Tell her how much you hated her for miscarrying your baby. He loves me, Journey! I'm the one giving him the gift of fatherhood," Lisa shouted. Fortunately, none of the guests heard the argument over the music.

Journey couldn't believe her ears. How could Lisa have been so kind to her the day she ran into her at the nail salon just for her to be nasty to her now?

Lisa was in the wrong all along; she was jealous of Journey because of Lance's loyalty. It took the miscarriage and a year of Lisa's persistence for Lance to sleep with her on a drunken night.

Avery gasped, but not before uppercutting Lisa right underneath her chin. Lance pulled Avery away while Carla ran to Lisa's aid.

"Avery, what's wrong with you? She's pregnant!" Journey screamed.

"I don't care; she had it coming," Avery said unapologetically.

Journey and Lance walked Avery to the parking lot, directly outside the main door.

Lance apologized to Journey; "Journ, I am so sorry."

Tears rolled down Journey's face as she remained speechless.

Avery chimed in, "We should go, Journey." Journey nodded her head in agreement.

As Avery walked Journey to her car, Joey ran after her.

With his hands on his knees and bending over to catch his breath, Joey asked Journey if she was OK.

Journey nodded and asked, "How is Lisa?"

"She'll be fine. It's about time someone gave her a taste of her own medicine. But I think it's an unspoken rule that you shouldn't put your hands on a pregnant woman," Joey said jokingly, motioning toward Avery.

Avery grinned. She would do anything in defense of Journey, no matter the circumstance.

They didn't return to the baby shower or feel welcomed after what happened. Avery sped out of the parking lot while Journey sat in her vehicle, catching her breath. Joey said goodbye to Journey and went back inside.

Before Journey drove off, Lance came over to her car and asked about her relationship with Joey. He accused Journey of having feelings for Joey.

Lance had been watching Journey interact with him. He felt a little jealous of how Journey and Joey spoke to one another. The smile that spread across Journey's face while she was talking to Joey made Lance angry.

Lance pushed through his anger and pleaded with Journey as his hands rested on her open window. The weather was still frigid, but Lance didn't care.

"I still want to be with you, Journey. Please give me another chance. We can start slow. Maybe we can grab something to eat next weekend. You are carrying my baby, and I want to be there for you and the baby."

"OK, Lance. We will see how next weekend goes. Bye." Journey put the window up and drove out of the parking lot.

Lance stood there watching her leave with a big smile on his face.

CHAPTER 7

After a good night's sleep, Journey woke up early, around eight, and made herself a small breakfast with tea on the side. Journey woke up feeling like she needed to make it right with her parents. She'd had enough time and space away from them, and she truly missed them. Journey dialed Nya's number, and the phone rang twice before Nya answered.

"Hey, Journ. How are you?"

"Hey, Ny. I think I am ready."

"Ready for what?" Nya asked.

"To talk to Mom and Dad."

"Oh wow. Are you sure?" Nya questioned.

"Yes, it needs to happen. It is long overdue," Journey declared.

"Do you want me to go with you?" Nya wondered.

"Yes, please," said Journey.

Nya showed up at Journey's apartment after stopping to check on her restaurant, which was nearby. They then drove together and showed up at their parents' house uninvited. When Journey made up her mind about something, she just did it . . . no phone calls or heads-ups were necessary.

When Mama Luna opened the front door, she and Journey locked eyes. Tears began falling from Mama Luna's face.

"Who is at the door, honey?" Dad asked from a distance.

"It's Journ!" Mama Luna yelled without taking her eyes off Journey.

"OK, this is awkward. Can we come in?" Nya interrupted.

"Oh yes, come in!" Mama Luna said as she moved aside to let the girls in.

Their dad slowly descended the upstairs; both parents appeared to be walking on eggshells because they didn't want to upset Journey in any way. They felt guilty for not telling Journey about Uncle Ernie, but their love for Journey had fueled that decision.

Sometimes, parents make decisions in the heat of the moment to protect their children, but later those decisions may backfire.

Everyone sat at the dining room table in anticipation. Journey and Nya were on one side of the table, and their parents were on the other. Judging by the look on their parents' faces, they expected Journey to give them a piece of her mind, but it was the complete opposite.

Journey started, "I have been doing a lot of thinking. I am not going to lie; I was shattered when Nya told me everything about Uncle Ernie. What hurt the most was the fact you two kept it from me for years. And you let him be around me; that made me furious. But Nya explained that you two did it out of love, and she told me how much this whole situation affected you two over the years. I forgive you."

There wasn't a dry eye at that dining room table.

Her dad got up and hugged Journey so tight that Nya had to separate them. He had been holding that anguish inside for a long time, and hugging Journey helped alleviate the tension he didn't know he had. Mama Luna wiped her eyes and blew her nose. She got up to hug Journey as well. It was a gentle and loving hug.

Nya broke the sympathy in the air. "Now that that's over with, what do you have to eat in there, Ma?" Nya motioned toward the kitchen.

Journey laughed at Nya's randomness. While wiping her tears and smiling with a peaceful ambiance surrounding them, Journey said to her parents, "You two are going to be grandparents again!"

"Now, why would you go and hit them with that news right after Ma finally stopped crying?" Nya asked jokingly.

Tears and praises to God began immediately. Journey had struggled to get pregnant, and when she finally got pregnant, she miscarried. Journey never thought she could have kids.

To see the ways God made was miraculous, and Journey set aside her anger toward Lance, Lisa, and whatever had a hold on her. Journey refused to be bound again. She was reminded of who she was and God's favor on her life. He had made a way out of no way, and Journey and her family were grateful. For the first time since Journey learned that she was pregnant, she was genuinely happy and excited to be a mother. She would not let Lance's actions and betrayal define her or her capabilities. If Journey wanted to give Lance another chance, that was her decision and no one else's.

After everyone had finished praying to God and enjoying each other's company, Mama Luna asked, "How far along are you?"

"Twelve weeks."

"Oh, praise God! That's wonderful."

Journey spent the next few hours enjoying the company of her family. They laughed and ate. Mama Luna brought out old photo albums with pictures of Nya, Journey, and Zelle when they were growing up. Journey loved anything that produced nostalgia and always enjoyed reminiscing.

When Journey and Nya finally left, the atmosphere felt lighter. Nya and Journey sat in silence for the duration of their car ride; they were socially and emotionally exhausted.

The weekend went by fast. With the eventful baby shower on Saturday and Journey spending time with her parents and Nya on Sunday, she was ready to return to the office. She looked forward to having a predictable routine. Going to work provided the structure that Journey could count on.

Journey woke up Monday morning and dressed in a pin-striped, two-piece suit with black Louboutins. She even added a bit more makeup than usual. When Journey finally arrived at work, she was in a good mood. She greeted everyone as she walked in. Journey typically greeted everyone, but that day, she did it out of cheer, not obligation. The past weekend had shown her a lot, and she felt at ease about where her life was headed. She was more excited about being pregnant now that her parents knew, and she had someone to share the excitement with. Journey felt good that the tables had turned with Lance. His chasing her made her feel good because it meant she could do what she thought was best and on her terms.

When Journey was comfortably seated in her black office chair, she decided to shoot Lance a text message:

> Journey: "Hey, are you free for dinner tonight?"
> Lance: "Yes, of course!"
> Journey: "OK, see you then. Around seven; you choose the place. Surprise me!"
> Lance: "Will do, Journ. :)"

Journey put her phone away with a big smile. When she looked up, she saw Joey standing at her office door.

"What are you so happy about? You're grinning from ear to ear," Joey said with a grin of his own.

"Oh, nothing. It was just Lance," Journey said with a shrug.

Joey's grin turned into a frown. Then, so did Journey's.

"What?" Journey asked.

Joey began pacing around the room then finally said, "Nothing. It's just that after all that happened at the baby shower, I am surprised you're speaking to him."

"I have to forgive him, Joey. He apologized. You heard what he said; it was a one-night stand. It didn't mean anything. Lisa is crazy."

"I suppose you're right," he continued. "I guess I'm just surprised. I thought you were a no-tolerance kind of woman. For as long as I have known you, you've always been stronger than that."

Journey was speechless. What could she say to that? Was the path of forgiveness a sign of weakness, or was she blind to Lance's transgressions?

Joey excused himself from Journey's office, and Journey could tell that Joey was disappointed.

That was a weird reaction. I didn't think he cared so much.

She never cared about people's opinions, but it didn't sit right with her when someone questioned her reputation and morals.

That interaction shifted Journey's mood. When Joey left her office, she slumped in her chair and stared at the ceiling for several moments. She had to snap out of her state of mind because she had work to do.

Journey sat up straight and started by opening and responding to important emails. She had court at the end of the week, so she had to prepare for that.

Now that Journey was pregnant, she didn't look forward to going to court like before, which was surprising because that had been one of Journey's favorite things to do. She loved her clients and always enjoyed a win and the opportunity to keep someone out of jail, but something had changed when she found out about the baby.

It was almost as if nothing else mattered but the baby. Journey had spent her whole life making sure everyone else was taken care of, from family to friends to clients. Maybe it was time for her to be a little selfish for the sake of her baby.

Journey was trying to wrap up as many cases as she could so she could focus on her health.

Later that night, Journey and Lance met for dinner, and they had an amazing time. It felt like a fresh new start. The conversation was fun; they reminisced about the times in college and why they had fallen in love with each other all those years ago. When the food arrived, Lance took a moment to carefully examine Journey.

"You look so beautiful tonight," he said with a huge smile.

Journey started to blush, "Thank you," she said as she sipped her strawberry lemonade.

"Journ, I feel horrible for what I did to you. I am so sorry. Losing you made me realize how much I love you. When I thought I might lose you forever, I knew I had to try to win you and your trust back."

Journey took Lance's confession to heart, and she was grateful. She felt God was giving her another chance to get what she wanted.

The dinner went so well that Journey invited Lance back to her apartment. As Journey unlocked the front door, she and Lance began playfully kissing. They made their way to the couch and continued kissing and cuddling one another. When the two came up for air, Lance continued to apologize. Journey saw the genuine sadness in Lance's eyes. She searched his eyes before she said, "I forgive you."

Journey didn't want the night to end. She was lost in blissful romance and wanted to live in this fairytale forever. The two fell asleep, but Lance woke up in the middle of the night, which caused Journey to wake up.

"Sorry, babe. I had to use the bathroom. I should also probably head out. I have to be at the office early tomorrow."

"No worries," said Journey.

Journey walked Lance to the front door. They kissed, and Lance disappeared into the hallway. Journey tried to go back to sleep but couldn't. She felt excited—excited for a new beginning, for another chance, for a father for her child.

Journey stayed awake until her alarm went off at seven. She swung her legs off her bed onto the fluffy rug beneath her feet.

She turned the tea kettle on and washed her face until she heard the kettle whistle.

She put on a casual outfit with some simple flats. She was at the stage of her pregnancy when she no longer wanted to wear heels. Being in heels all day was uncomfortable, especially since Journey had to be on her feet.

* * * * * *

When Journey walked into the office, she saw that Joey was waiting for her. They hadn't spoken since that uncomfortable conversation about Lance.

"Hey, Joey. Is everything OK?" Journey asked cautiously.

Joey turned from facing Journey's desk to face her. "Hey, um, Journ. I have something I wanted to talk to you about."

"Wassup?"

"So, the divorce is finalized."

"Oh, how are you feeling?" Journey asked, taken aback.

"I feel great!" Joey said distractedly. But he continued, "Because the divorce is finalized, I feel like now I can say this. Journey, I really admire you. You are ambitious, kind, caring, and beautiful. I've kind of always had a crush on you, and leaving Carla made me realize how much I want to explore a relationship with you. I was taken aback when I heard that you were talking to Lance again."

Journey took a moment to process everything Joey had just said. But before she could respond, there was a knock at her office door. She saw through the fishbowl glass that it was Lance, and he was holding flowers.

Joey quickly got up and said, "Oh, I will leave you two alone." He rushed out of Journey's office. When Joey was gone, Journey waved Lance to come in. His smile quickly faded.

"What is going on with you two?" Lance asked, tight-lipped.

"What? Nothing," Journey said carelessly.

"I don't want you talking to him," Lance said firmly with an underlying tone of anger.

"Well, Lance, we work together. That is kind of impossible," Journey replied with a chuckle.

Lance grabbed Journey's chin with some pressure. "This isn't funny; I mean it. If I see you talking to him again, I am going to hurt him."

"OK," said Journey in defeat and fear. In all her years with Lance, she had never witnessed this type of behavior, and she didn't know how to react.

Lance stormed out with the flowers still in hand.

Journey was sick when she saw Joey shaking his head from the hallway. He had witnessed the whole thing.

CHAPTER 8

Two months later

Things between Journey and Lance continued to go well. They were hanging out more, and a few days a week, Lance would spend the night at Journey's apartment. In addition, Journey had been away from the office more as she and Lance would grab lunch weekly. She began falling behind at work, which wasn't like her.

Joey had to consult with Journey on certain cases that the firm handled. Sometimes, their interactions would be awkward because Journey felt there were still unspoken feelings lingering in the air. Although Carla was Journey's assistant, Journey allowed Carla to assist other attorneys at the firm since Journey's caseload was minimal as of late. It was also a good excuse to stay away from Carla after what happened at the baby shower. Joey mentioned in passing that Carla didn't blame her for what Avery did. But it was still awkward to see Carla around the office.

Now that Journey was more than halfway through her pregnancy, she wasn't handling court cases. She continued to consult on cases but spread out her caseload among the other attorneys at the firm.

When lunchtime rolled around, Lance texted Journey to inquire about lunch:

> Lance: "Hey! Are we still on for lunch today? I figured we could try this new Mexican restaurant in Yonkers."
> Journey: "Yonkers? Babe, that is an hour round trip. I have work to do. I don't think I can commit that much time. I only get forty-five minutes for lunch."
> Lance: "If you don't want to go with me, just say that."
> Journey: "No, babe; I want to go with you."
> Lance: "OK; love you. :)"

After Journey saw Lance's last text, she began finishing up some work that had to be done by the end of the day.

Suddenly, Journey's phone rang. It was her mom.

Mom never calls me in the middle of a workday.

Journey held her phone to her ear. "Hello. Wassup, Ma?" Journey heard crying on the other end of the line.

"Ma, what's wrong?" Journey pleaded.

"It's your uncle. He had a heart attack, and he is not doing well. We are all going to see him at the hospital."

"Oh . . . um, how's Dad?" Journey asked while trying to remain calm.

"He's not doing well, Journ. I need you to come. Please," Mama Luna begged.

"Of course," Journey said as she hung up the phone.

Journey felt as though someone had smacked her in the face. She had just forgiven her parents, and she had somewhat forgiven her uncle, but not to his face. But knowing that

Uncle Ernie was not doing well made it imperative that Journey forgive him while there was still time. She wished she had more time . . . she wished she had treated the situation differently.

Journey told her colleagues she had a family emergency and needed to go. She assured them that she would get the paperwork to them before the end of the day.

Before Journey left, she texted Lance to let him know she couldn't meet for lunch because Uncle Ernie was hospitalized. After she hit send, she immediately called Nya.

Nya answered on the first ring. "Hey, Journ. I just heard what happened. How are you feeling?"

"Honestly, I am shocked. I don't know how to feel. I feel bad for Dad, but I feel nothing toward Uncle Ernie right now."

"That's understandable. I am about to head over to the hospital now. Do you want me to pick you up on my way?"

"Yeah, that would be helpful. Just pick me up from work."

After Journey hung up with Nya, she just sat in front of her work building, waiting. She didn't look at her phone; she was idle. All she could do was picture how her interaction with her uncle would go. Would it lead to chaos, or would it be a peaceful encounter?

Nya pulled up in her black BMW X5 and let the driver's window down. "Journey!" she shouted.

Journey was lost in a cloud of her own thoughts. When she realized it was Nya, she smiled and ran toward the car. Journey was happy to see Nya. With her being so busy at work lately, it was nice to see her—not under these circumstances, but nonetheless, she was thankful that she and Nya were together.

On the ride to the hospital, Nya and Journey vented their emotions and shared how they would feel if Uncle Ernie died. Their main concern was for their dad and whether he was OK and how he would react if his only brother died.

They finally arrived at the hospital, and Zelle was the one who came down to greet Nya and Journey. The hospital smelled stale—like ending times or new beginnings. Journey never liked hospitals. Even for her prenatal checkups, she wanted to get in and out as quickly as possible.

"Hey, Sis. You're getting big," Zelle said with a chuckle.

Journey punched Zelle in the arm for that comment, but then she started to giggle.

Nya asked, "How is everything up there, Zelle?"

"Eh, not good. Uncle Ernie is in and out of consciousness; the doctors say that his heart is so weak that they don't expect him to make it through the night."

What Zelle said left Journey and Nya distraught but also prepared. They all walked toward Uncle Ernie's room; Zelle led the way.

When they arrived, the first thing they saw was Cousin Pamela weeping in the corner. Their dad was sitting right next to the bed where Uncle Ernie lay. Several tubes and machines were connected to Uncle Ernie's mouth and chest.

He awoke with a deep, gravelly cough. The first person he spotted was Journey. This time Journey didn't feel squirmy; she felt sorrow and sadness for him. Lying in that hospital bed, he was finally vulnerable. He wasn't an aggressor; he was defenseless.

"Journey? You came? I didn't think you'd come when your mom spoke with you," Uncle Ernie said softly, mostly struggling to breathe.

Journey said awkwardly, "Yeah, of course!"

"I may not get this opportunity again. I wanted to apologize."

"Apologize for what?" Journey asked. Uncle Ernie had never apologized, so Journey was genuinely curious as to what he was saying sorry for.

"You know what—the assault and trauma I placed upon you at such a young age. I can tell by the way you look at me that it has bothered you all these years."

Nya could see her dad stop crying and ball up his fist. The hashing of the past was too much for him at that moment. Nya discreetly pulled him to the side so that he wouldn't cause a scene and so that Journey and Uncle Ernie could see face-to-face.

Before Journey could respond or react, Uncle Ernie mustered up enough strength to tell everyone in the room a story. But it was as if the story was only for Journey.

He started, "When Romero and I were eight and ten, we had this babysitter named Laurel; she was in college. We loved her. She would take us to the park, read us bedtime stories, and make the best lasagna," Uncle Ernie said recalling the pleasant memories.

He continued, "Then, one night, she touched me, and it didn't feel right. But she told me it was OK; she said I was safe. I won't get into details, but the sexual abuse lasted years until she graduated from college and moved back to Vermont. I was in pain for a very long time. I didn't know how to deal with that pain. I am so sorry. I can never forgive myself for hurting you girls." Uncle Ernie said through muffled sobs.

While Uncle Ernie was crying, Journey grabbed his hand. She looked him in the eyes and smiled. Journey's eyes told Uncle Ernie that she forgave him, and he received it. They hugged one another while the rest of the room sat in silence until Journey's dad interrupted, "Ernie, why didn't you tell me? How did I not know?" He sounded upset but also hurt.

"I wanted to shield you from it. I didn't want you to be hurt," said Uncle Ernie.

Journey did not know whether her wounds had healed or reopened, but she felt good and hoped everyone else did.

When everyone realized Uncle Ernie was doing better and breathing normally, they decided it was a good time to pray. Nya grabbed Zelle's hand while Mama Luna and Dad joined hands, which left Cousin Pamela, Uncle Ernie, and Journey to unite their hands in prayer. Zelle led a prayer that specifically asked God to heal Uncle Ernie and strengthen the family. Everyone said what they wanted God to do. Then, in unison, they began to recite the Lord's prayer.

After prayer, Journey hugged Cousin Pamela, and she reciprocated with a heartfelt hug of her own. She cried in Journey's arms.

"Why are you crying, Pammy? I am going to be fine. God heard our prayers," Uncle Ernie said with a smile.

Shortly after, everyone said their goodbyes. They felt good about Uncle Ernie and promised to visit him the following day.

Zelle and Journey caught a ride with Nya, but Cousin Pam, Mama Luna, and Dad decided to stay a little while longer since Uncle Ernie was full of energy and enjoying their company.

Being heavily pregnant, Journey was starving. "Can we go to McDonalds?"

"I'm down," Zelle screamed from the back seat.

"Yeah, sure. We can go before I stop at the restaurant, Nya added."

"On second thought," Journey said, "we can grab some food at your restaurant. I will order. What do you want, Zelle?"

"Hmm, let me get some rasta pasta with jerk chicken and a piece of orange glazed cake."

"I should've known," Journey said laughing. "Do you want anything, Ny?"

"Ordering from my own restaurant is weird," Nya commented. "But I will take the same thing Zelle ordered."

"All right, I just ordered three plates of rasta pasta and two pieces of cake."

The drive from the hospital to the restaurant took at least forty-five minutes. On the way to the restaurant, Zelle fell asleep in the backseat while Nya and Journey talked about the details of Journey's baby shower, which was just around the corner. Nya was planning the whole thing, but Journey, with her controlling nature, had to have a say in some of the major components.

They finally arrived at Nya's restaurant, "The August." When Nya parked, Zelle instantly woke up. Nya quickly got out of the car and ran inside the restaurant; she had some small things to take care of, so she went inside and grabbed the food for everyone.

While Nya was inside, Journey finally looked at her phone for the first time in several hours since she left the office. To her surprise, she found that she had eleven missed calls and eighteen text messages from Lance. But what caught her eye were the two missed calls from Joey and three missed calls from the firm.

Oh no, I forgot to send the documentation for one of our immigration clients. Today was the deadline, and I totally lost track of time.

Journey immediately called Joey back. Whatever was going on, she figured that she'd much rather hear it from him than one of the firm's partners.

The phone rang five times before Joey answered. "Hey, Journey! Where have you been? We have all been calling you."

"I know, I'm sorry. I had a family emergency. What's going on?" Journey asked.

"Oh no! Is everything OK?" Joey changed his tone to worry.

"Yeah. Everything is fine now. My uncle had a heart attack, and we were worried. But he is doing better."

"Oh, that's good to hear. But anyway, Journey, we have been getting calls from the immigration client. Because we didn't file in time, they may never be able to come to this country for work."

"Oh, no, I didn't realize their work visa was contingent upon this paperwork."

"Journ, we've had meetings about this for weeks. You just haven't been around. Your lunch breaks have been getting longer and longer. The only way that we can reapply is if the representing attorney, which is you, gets disbarred. This is not like you, Journey; you better pray the partners don't let you go. It's a bad look for the firm."

Journey didn't know whether to be defensive or not. But underneath it all, she was hurt and devastated. She'd never been fired from a job, and she had always been the highest-performing attorney at Johnson & Associates. What was she doing?

The pregnancy hormones kicked in, and Journey couldn't help but cry. She sobbed, "I know I didn't submit the work on time. But there must be something we can do, right?"

Joey interjected, "I didn't mean to upset you, Journ. I just know what a great attorney you are, and I hate seeing this happen to you. I will make some calls and see what I can do."

"No, no; it's not your fault. It's mine. I will talk to you later, OK?"

"OK, get some rest. It will be OK," Joey said calmly.

Journey hung up the phone and sat still, looking defeated. She wasn't even hungry anymore; the conversation with Joey had ruined her appetite.

Zelle peered into the rearview mirror from the backseat to see Journey. He placed his hand on her shoulders, and Journey's hands met his.

Nya finally returned to the car with the food, only to see that Zelle's and Journey's eyes were red. When Nya saw that both of them had been crying, she reached out to Journey before sharing her own news.

"What happened, Journ?" Nya asked.

"I might get disbarred. I forgot to submit some really important paperwork. I've been away from the office a lot lately, and . . ."

"Where have you been? You love your job, so why would you be away?" Nya asked.

"Lance and I have been spending more time together, and we have been grabbing lunch a few times a week for a little while."

Nya and Zelle shared a look.

Nya finally said, "Lance doesn't seem good for you, Journ."

"How could you say that? He loves me, and he is the father of my child," Journey said defensively.

Nya lifted her hands in surrender. "OK, it is your life. Your choice." Nya wasn't in the mood to prove a point or make Journey understand anything right now. She had news of her own. "Dad just called me. Uncle Ernie didn't make it; he died shortly after we left," Nya said quickly and without emotion.

"Oh no. Ugh, this is crazy. He was perfectly fine when we left," Journey said in shock with her hands over her mouth.

Zelle put his head in his lap and took a breath. Then he said calmly, "Maybe God took him while he was free from sin so he can be in heaven."

"Family is so important. We have to be there for Pam," Ny said.

Zelle and Journey nodded their heads in agreement.

CHAPTER 9

After being hit with bad news after bad news, Journey took a moment to look through her missed emails and messages. She saw Lance's most recent text messages first:

Lance: "You didn't want to go to lunch with me. Why did you have to lie about your uncle being in the hospital?!"
Lance: "Why aren't you answering?"
Lance: "Journey, stop playing with me. Answer your phone!"
Lance: "I bet you're with that Joey dude. Ima kill him!"

Journey, shocked by the text messages, decided to call Lance to find out what was going on. Lance answered on the first ring. "Journey, where are you?" he said in a concerned, worried tone.

"I'm with Zelle and Nya. On my way home."

"Why do you sound like you've been crying?" asked Lance. He sounded sweet and concerned.

Journey answered, "Yeah, well, I just spoke with Joey, and he told me I might get disbarred because I missed an important deadline."

Lance quickly interjected, "Joey! Why is he talking to you?! Didn't I tell you to stop speaking to him?"

Journey tried to speak quietly and kindly. "Babe, I might lose my license, and you're more concerned about Joey?"

Lance immediately hung up the phone.

Nya and Zelle heard Lance's raised voice through the phone. Nya looked at Zelle through the rearview mirror; she could see that Zelle was getting agitated. The last time she saw that look in Zelle's eyes, he was a teenager, a menace to the world. Nya mouthed "don't" to Zelle.

The air in the car was thick with a mixture of grief, frustration, and numbness. No one said a word, but Nya and Zelle exchanged looks. They continued to stay quiet until Nya pulled in front of Journey's apartment building. Zelle exited the car and offered to walk Journey upstairs, but Journey politely declined, "I'll be fine, Zelle. You two have a good night; I'll talk to you later. I may stop by Mom and Dad's to check on them. I will check on Pam tomorrow. I'm sure she needs her space." Journey vanished through the lobby doors.

Zelle and Nya sat in Nya's car in front of Journey's apartment building, eating their food and discussing what had just transpired. They were more concerned about Journey possibly getting disbarred than about Lance screaming at her on the phone.

"What the heck was that?" Nya asked blankly. "She just left like nothing happened."

"That's how Journey copes with things. But I don't like this dude. She's pregnant, and he has the nerve to yell at her like that? Nah, I'm going to have to talk to him. Teach him how to talk to my sister."

Any other time, Nya would object, but not this time. Nya didn't like how Lance treated Journey, and she didn't care what happened to him. Journey is her sister, and that means everything to Nya. She vowed to always protect her. Finally, Nya drove off.

Meanwhile, Journey settled into her apartment, threw her purse on the kitchen island, and plopped on the living room couch. Shortly after, there was a loud knock at her door.

Journey was too big to sit and get back up easily, so she was annoyed at whoever knocked on the door. She shuffled to the door and opened it, and she saw Lance, then his fist. Everything went dark.

Lance had stormed inside the apartment but not before sucker punching Journey in her right eye, which left her unconscious on the floor. While she was on the floor, Lance began to scream at her, "You're such a whore. I don't know why I tried to mend things with you. I should've left you! I hate you!"

Journey began waking up. She spotted Lance standing over her, and she immediately flinched. She was terrified; she had never seen him like this. The smell of alcohol spewed from his mouth with every breath. He spat at Journey, stormed out of the apartment, and slammed the door hard and loudly.

Journey was experiencing stomach pains and immediately thought about the baby. She managed to get herself up and walked to the bathroom to clean herself up. Journey felt a liquid substance dripping from her leg. *Dang, did I pee on myself?*

When she wiped herself, she realized it was blood on her legs. In a panic, she called Nya.

"Nya, pick up . . . pick up!" Journey said to herself.

Nya's phone went to voicemail.

Journey began to sob, but Nya called her back.

"Hey, Journ. Sorry, I was just dropping Zelle off at his house. Wassup? How are you feeling?"

"Nya, you have to come!" Journey said through constant sobs. "I'm bleeding. Can you take me to the emergency room? I'm worried about the baby. What if it's another miscarriage?"

"Oh my goodness, Journ, I'm on my way! I will be there in fifteen minutes!

"OK, I'll have the door unlocked, so just come in, OK?"

"Mm," Nya said, distracted and honking her horn.

* * * * * *

When Nya arrived at Journey's apartment, she was out of breath because she didn't have time to wait for the elevator. She needed to get to Journey.

She immediately caught her breath when she saw Journey. Journey was lying on the couch, holding her stomach, and breathing slowly.

"What happened to your face!"

"What do you mean?" Journey asked as she touched her face in confusion.

Nya snatched the hand mirror from the bathroom sink, shoved it in Journey's face, and demanded that Journey tell her what had happened.

Journey put her head down in shame. She hadn't realized that Lance's punch had left her with a black eye.

"Was this Lance?!?" Nya asked with an accusative tone.

"He didn't mean to," Journey pleaded.

"Don't piss me off, Journey. You're pregnant. Do you think it is okay . . . for him to hit you?"

Journey didn't answer.

Agitated, Nya hurried Journey. "Let's go."

On the way to the emergency room, neither Journey nor Nya said a word.

Zelle called, and Nya answered by car play.

"Hey! Me and the fam just arrived at Mom and Dad's house. Y'all should come by. I tried to call Journey, but she didn't answer her phone."

Journey looked at Nya and whispered, "Please don't tell him. Don't tell him I'm with you."

Nya responded to Zelle, "Um . . . yeah. I'll see if I can make it over. I have stuff I have to wrap up at the restaurant. I'll call you when I'm finished."

"OK, Sis. Love you. Bye"

As Nya hung up the phone, she turned and made a face. Nya never liked lying, but she did it to protect Journey.

Journey pleaded, "You can't tell Zelle what happened. He would literally kill Lance."

Nya kept her mouth shut and kept driving. The emergency room was nearly empty when they arrived, and Journey was immediately checked in. Journey and Nya waited about twenty minutes for a doctor to come and check on Journey.

"What brings you in here today?" asked the doctor.

"I fell, and now I'm bleeding. I have a history of miscarrying, so I want to make sure everything is OK."

Nya sucked her breath in through her teeth and mumbled under her breath, but Journey shot her a look, and Nya composed herself.

"OK, let's take a quick ultrasound to make sure the baby is all right, and after that, we will draw some blood to ensure you are OK." The doctor continued, "All right, I am going to tilt the bed all the way back, and I ask that you lift up your shirt a little. This will be cold," the doctor said as he applied ultrasound gel to Journey's abdomen.

The doctor applied the wand to Journey's stomach. After numerous attempts, the doctor struggled to find a heartbeat. "Hmm, the heartbeat is unusually hard to find."

"What does that mean?" Journey asked, worried.

"It means that the heartbeat may not be present. I am unable to hear one," the doctor said in confusion as he stared at the ultrasound monitor.

"There it is!" shouted the doctor.

Journey and Nya both let out a sigh of relief.

"The baby was a little stressed, but she's OK."

"She? It's a girl? Journey looked at Nya with tears in her eyes.

"All the other times I got an ultrasound, the legs were crossed," Journey told the doctor.

Journey was so excited, and she realized she had to stay away from Lance for the baby's sake and for her own sake. This was Journey's wake-up call.

Zelle called Nya again as she and Journey were wrapping up in the ER.

"Nya, are you coming?"

"Eh, I don't think so. I am going to spend some time with Journ; she isn't feeling well."

"Oh . . . OK. Well, I will come over too," Zelle said.

Nya looked at Journey with raised eyebrows while she held the phone to her ear.

"What?" Journey whispered.

Nya shook her head, brushing off Journey, and responded to Zelle, "Okay, cool. I'll let Journey know."

Nya and Journey rushed into Journey's apartment and tried to cover up Journey's black eye. They coated it with makeup, but the bruising was still noticeable. The girls gave up when they heard the knock at the door; it was Zelle.

While Nya ran to open the door, Journey positioned herself on the couch and faced the television. Journey lay on the couch with the bruised side of her face against a pillow.

"Hey, Journ. What's going on?" Zelle asked.

That question made Journey sob. She couldn't hide anything from her siblings.

"I'm broken up about Uncle Ernie. How could so much happen in one day? I'm broken up about the possibility of losing everything I have worked so hard to achieve."

At this point, Journey sat up on the couch, and Zelle clearly saw her face. Zelle reached over to touch Journey's eye; touching her made it real. Zelle pulled her into a tender embrace. But what started as a gentle embrace led to sheer anxiety and then anger; he knew exactly what had happened without asking.

Because Journey was visibly hurt, Zelle set aside his feelings and continued to embrace her with a hug that Nya later joined, which lasted what felt like forever.

Over the past few months, Journey had not fully noticed the sacrifices her family had made because they loved and supported her. In so many instances, Journey's family could have been selfish, placing their feelings front and center. But they did not, and Journey was grateful for a family that loved and supported each other like they did.

She had to face her firm the following day, and the sheer anxiety brought on by the day's festivities made Journey all the more exhausted.

By the next morning, the bruising under Journey's eye was less visible, and she was able to cover the discoloration with makeup. When Journey arrived at the office, the staff and her coworkers greeted her warmly as they always did. However, one of the firm's partners, Allison Johnson, was waiting in Journey's office. Journey's heart dropped when she saw her.

"Hey, Journey!" Allison said excitedly.

Her energy threw Journey off. Journey walked in slowly and awkwardly, barely able to say, "Hey . . ."

Once Journey was seated, Allison spoke firmly, "You have been a great asset to this firm since you joined, but there are attorneys here who feel you have been slacking on your duties. We understand you are pregnant and taking a lighter load, but not meeting critical deadlines is unacceptable, Journey, and we won't tolerate it. The partners and I have decided to place you on a two-week suspension while we figure out what to do about this most recent situation regarding your possible disbarment."

"Do I stay for the rest of the day or leave now?" Journey asked strongly.

"You can close out what you need to, but then you are welcome to leave. We will be in touch," Allison said as she stood up and walked out of Journey's office and into the chaos of daily operations. She left calmly as if she had not just delivered reckoning news.

Journey tried to remain strong without shedding a tear. She closed some cases and handed the rest to the secretary to be assigned to another attorney.

As Journey was gathering up her things, Joey snuck into her office.

"Hey, Journ. You OK? I heard what they planned to do today but thought they would have done it at the end of the day. I'm sorry, Journ."

"Don't be. This is on me, and I need to be held accountable."

"What has been going on with you? You've never missed a deadline," Joey asked.

"I guess I just have a lot going on and feel overwhelmed," Journey admitted.

"Why didn't you talk to me before it got to this point?"

Journey started sobbing. "I didn't realize until it was too late."

Joey hugged Journey, and Journey then scurried out of the office. She figured she should go to her parents' house to check on her dad. So she went home and changed into something more comfortable.

When Journey arrived at her parents' house, her mom was happy to see her, but she was also confused. She questioned why Journey was not at work, "Why are you over here in the middle of the afternoon? Did you not have work today?" Mama Luna asked.

"I finished all I needed to, so I figured I would come over and check on y'all, considering what happened last night," Journey said as she reached for a hug.

"Oh, well, I am happy to see you. Your dad is not doing well; he is in the living room lying on the couch."

Journey and her mom went into the living room; her dad was like a zombie. The sports channel was playing, but he wasn't watching.

"Hey, Dad. How are you feeling?"

He lifted his head quickly to the sound of Journey's voice. "Hey, Journ, how's it going? How's the baby?"

"The baby is good! Can't wait to meet her."

"Aww . . . it's a girl?!" He sat up quickly, and he rubbed Journey's belly. This news brought a smile to her parents' faces.

Mama Luna said, "You mentioned that you want to get a bigger place for you and the baby. So when do you want to go look at houses?"

"Yeah, I'm still interested. I was waiting for my bonus at work, but I don't think that will be happening," said Journey.

"Why not? You've been there for years; you're the best lawyer they have!" her dad said in a defensive tone.

"I think my career is over," Journey confessed.

CHAPTER 10

The day for the baby shower finally arrived, and Nya did not disappoint. The hall was covered in white and gold roses. The tables were decorated with beautiful princess-themed centerpieces. The lights that read "Sands Baby Girl" were gorgeous. Journey was truly in awe.

Journey's appearance had not changed much during the pregnancy; she didn't gain any face weight, and she was all belly. She wore a light pink off-the-shoulder gown that cutely highlighted her belly and crystal-studded sandals to ensure that her swollen feet were comfortable.

The baby shower was scheduled for three thirty, and guests started to arrive around four. Journey greeted all her guests, most of whom were family, and then Avery walked in.

"Avery! Oh my goodness!" Journey ran into Avery's arms and gave her a tight hug. Well, the tightest hug she could give with the belly in the way.

Avery's complexion was darker than usual, and she looked beautiful. Her eyes glistened; she wore her hair up in a bun composed of a month-old knotless braid set.

"Hi, Journ! You didn't think I would miss your big day, did you?" Avery snickered.

"Actually, I did; you've been gone for weeks. I wasn't sure if you would make it back in time," said Journey. "Dang girl, you got tan! I take it that your time in the Bahamas was good for you. I feel like I haven't seen you in forever."

"Yes! It's been weeks. It was so nice to see my family, but what did I miss while I was gone?"

"Girl, how long do you have?" Journey said while grabbing Avery's arm.

Avery could tell that something was off. There was a bit of sorrow in Journey's eyes.

Avery and Journey were suddenly interrupted, "Hey, Avery!" Nya screamed from afar.

Nya had been setting up the buffet table when she noticed Journey talking to Avery. Since Nya's restaurant catered for the baby shower, Nya had to ensure that everything looked perfect.

"Hey, Ny, what's going on?"

"It's good to see you. I see you enjoyed your trip," Nya said with a smile.

"Yeah, yeah, it was nice, but I'm glad to be back with you all," said Avery.

"Come, Avery. I need some help getting the rest of the food."

Nya pulled Avery's arm, and they disappeared through the double doors leading to the parking lot. Journey was left alone and tasked with greeting everyone.

Guests began flooding in, and Journey's parents and Zelle finally arrived. Once they arrived, Journey felt much better. She was getting tired, so she sat down at the table closest to her. Everyone was trying to get a picture with her, and they wanted to touch Journey's belly, which she was opposed to. Mama Luna always told Journey and her siblings to not let anyone touch their hair or belly when they were pregnant. Journey took that as no one should ever touch her; she didn't like to be touched.

Soon, it was time for Journey to open her gifts in front of a room full of people, which she was uncomfortable doing by herself. Lance never showed up, and she was confused about why that was. Lance's parents had shown up to the baby shower around five; they asked Journey if she had seen Lance.

Lance's mom, Brenda, loved Journey and wouldn't miss this day for the world. So, she was disappointed to learn that her son had not shown up and wasn't taking care of his responsibility as the child's father.

Of course, Journey's family was livid that Lance didn't show up. But they knew not to let Journey know they were upset. She didn't need any more stress, but boy, was Zelle ready to find Lance.

Nya, being the attuned sister, noticed that Journey looked uncomfortable, so Nya went up to the front with Journey to assist her with opening gifts. Avery was not too far behind. They both wanted to support Journey in her time of need.

When the baby shower was over, Journey was ready to go home and rest. Baby shower duties take a toll on expectant mothers; it's a taxing commitment. Avery dropped Journey off at her apartment and waited for her to enter the building before driving away.

Journey's phone was in her purse the whole evening. When she finally got to her apartment, she looked at her phone and found five missed calls and three text messages from Joey. One of the text messages caught her eye. It said, "Hey, Journey! Call me. I have some great news!"

Journey's suspension had lasted longer than the original timeline of two weeks. She had been out of work for exactly three weeks and three days. Journey was hoping that Joey's good news had something to do with her job.

Journey's excitement gave her a burst of energy. As Journey began to click Joey's name on her contact list, there was a knock at the door. Journey placed her phone on the counter and walked two steps to the door.

Ugh, who could this be?

Journey peeked through the peephole. Of course, it was Lance. Journey opened the door, and Lance immediately began pleading.

"I'm so sorry, Journey. I didn't mean to put my hands on you. It will never happen again."

She was hesitant to let him inside the apartment until Lance said, "Please, Journey, I need you. I lost my job a couple of weeks ago. Lisa had the baby, and she just told me that the kid is not mine. I am not okay right now, and I need you, Journ. That's why I wasn't at the baby shower. I'm so sorry."

All this fuss for nothing.

Journey's big heart couldn't take it; she let Lance in and hugged him while he sobbed. The smell of liquor coming from Lance's mouth penetrated Journey's nostrils.

Lance must have really fallen if he turned to drinking. He never enjoyed drinking, not even a glass of wine.

As the hug persisted, Lance noticed Journey's phone on the kitchen counter. Her screen was still showing Joey's contact info.

Suddenly, Lance's whole mood changed. He pushed Journey away from him and began pacing back and forth.

"What?" Journey asked in confusion. "Did I do something to upset you?"

"Do you think I am stupid, Journey!" Lance screamed, looking directly at her.

Journey began to stutter, "Wha . . . what?"

Lance grabbed Journey's phone and flaunted it in her face, "Why do you love to disrespect me? Why are you still talking to this dude?"

Joey's name and number were clearly visible on the phone's screen.

"He was calling me about —"

Before Journey could finish her sentence, she felt Lance's big but dry hands gripping her neck.

"Stop lying!" Lance screamed at the top of his lungs. The anger only tightened Lance's grip on Journey's neck.

"Lance, I can't breathe," Journey cried before losing consciousness for a moment.

When Lance realized what he had done, he ran to Journey's aid and started apologizing, kissing, and hugging her. "I promise I'll get help. I will go to rehab, therapy, whatever you want!"

"It's not about what I want; it is about what you know to be right," Journey said matter-of-factly.

Journey was so numb and exhausted that she just let him hold her and apologize. When they eventually went to the bedroom to lie down, Lance fell asleep as soon as his head hit the pillow. But Journey stayed awake and stared at the ceiling, wondering how she had gotten here—staying in an abusive relationship. Was that something Journey wanted?

Journey mustered up the courage to call Lance's mom, Brenda. She told Miss Brenda all about Lance's addiction and what had been going on.

Lance's parents immediately came to Journey's apartment. Lance was still asleep. Miss Brenda and her husband Mr. Sam turned the bedroom lights on and shook Lance. When Lance jerked awake, Miss Brenda began confronting him.

Lance looked at Journey with an expression that said he felt so betrayed. Journey turned away and walked into the kitchen. But she still heard the conversation in the bedroom.

"While pregnant? That is completely unacceptable. How could you, Lance? I am so heartbroken and so disappointed. You most certainly weren't raised like this," Miss Brenda said.

Lance's dad interrupted and firmly said, "You are going to rehab. Get your stuff; let's go."

Seeing Lance escorted out by his parents made him look so small. At that moment, he was a child, not the man Journey had known all these years.

Miss Brenda and Mr. Sam hugged Journey goodbye and went into the hallway. After she closed the door, she ran to grab her phone. Among other things, Journey's need to know Joey's news kept her up.

Journey suddenly realized that it was nearly midnight. Although she felt it was inconsiderate to call at that hour, she didn't care. She called Joey anyway.

"Hello," said Joey in a raspy tone.

"Hey, Joey, I'm sorry I'm calling so late. The baby shower was today, and I missed your calls. What is the good news?"

Journey could hear Joey tossing and turning in his bed. "Um . . . yeah, give me a second."

Journey chuckled to herself.

"So, I was calling you because I contacted my old law school buddy and got some news on your case."

"Oh, nice. What did he say?" Journey asked.

"Ah, sorry I'm stretching the story out, but he was able to make this whole thing go away. He reached out to Allison already, so you're good to go. I know your maternity leave starts in a couple of weeks. It seems like perfect timing."

"Oh, my goodness, Joey! I am so grateful; thank you so much! I was sure that my career was over." Journey shouted while jumping for joy. "This is such good news," cried Journey. "There's been so much going on, and I truly needed this news."

"Oh no, Journey," Joey said with sympathy. "What's been going on?"

Journey couldn't control her emotions, and she bared everything. She felt comfortable sharing with Joey.

"Well, first, my uncle died a couple of weeks ago, and Lance hasn't been making this pregnancy easy for me," Journey admitted.

"Oh no. I'm so sorry to hear that, Journey. I know you had to leave that day because your uncle was in the hospital, but I didn't know that he passed away. How are you feeling?"

"Yeah, the funeral services were last weekend, so my family and I have started the grieving process. I am OK. I'm more worried about my dad; that was his only sibling."

"Well, I am glad you're doing OK. You said Lance hasn't been making your pregnancy easy. What do you mean?" asked Joey.

"Well, he hasn't been nice to me lately. He hates that I speak to you. You are the center of most of our arguments," Journey informed Joey.

It slipped out. Journey was always told to keep family business in the family. But she couldn't help herself.

Joey responded, "Journey, was that why he left the office so suddenly that day?"

"Yes, I guess. I don't remember," Journey continued. "Can you keep a secret?"

"I am a lawyer. I would hope so," Joey joked.

Journey chuckled, "No, but for real."

"Hit me," Joey tempted.

"After Lance put his hands on me the first time, I thought I was supposed to forgive him. Everything happened so fast. I had to go to the ER to check on the baby because I was bleeding," she explained.

Joey was quiet and let Journey continue.

"Then, when he choked me unconscious earlier, I sat in bed beside him like nothing happened. I knew something had to give," said Journey.

"He hit you more than once? Journey . . . because I care for you so much, I will not say what I want. A part of me wants to kill him. What kind of sick person hits a woman, especially when she is carrying his child?"

"You know what the worst part is? I took him back because I thought that's what I wanted. I wanted my kid to have a two-parent family, and I didn't want to raise a kid alone."

"Yeah, that's why the Bible tells us to lean not on our own understanding. We can be blinded by emotions and not see what God has for us."

"I didn't know you were into God," Journey said, impressed and intrigued.

"Yeah! I go to church every Sunday. I grew up in a Pentecostal church."

"I often thought to myself, 'God, what did I do wrong? You tell us to forgive those who have wronged us.' I forgave Lance. Why is our relationship not how it used to be? He isn't what he used to be. He has the spirit of jealousy and control on him."

"Yes, but does God say that you must endure the abuse, the lies, and the unfaithfulness? You can forgive, but it doesn't mean stay."

Journey was speechless.

CHAPTER 11

"Push, push! Come on, Journey, you can do it!" yelled Avery and Nya in unison.

Journey's parents decided to stay in the waiting room. Mama Luna did not like blood or screaming, and Journey's dad was patient and didn't mind waiting.

Avery and Nya jumped at the opportunity to be a part of the birthing experience with Journey.

"I am! It hurts!" Journey screamed.

"The head is almost out. Keep going, Journ!" Nya shouted excitedly, keeping her eyes glued on her sister pushing out her niece.

With one last push, Isabella Joy Sands made her entrance into the world. Her cry lit up the room. Weighing six pounds three ounces, she was the perfect size. She had a head full of black curls, just like her momma, and a deep dimple on her left cheek. She was born on a beautiful June morning at 7:03 a.m. The weather fit the occasion.

After the doctors cleaned Isabella, they placed her on Journey's bare chest. Tears streamed down Journey's face as she was in complete awe. Avery stood by admiring Journey and her strength while Nya went to get Mama Luna, her dad, and Zelle.

In that very moment, something changed in Journey. Nothing else mattered—not Lance and not work; all that mattered was the baby in her arms. A breeze of gratefulness swept through Journey. She had never experienced this type of peace.

Journey had always wanted to be a mother, and after having difficulty getting pregnant and two miscarriages, Journey had lost hope. But now that she could hold her baby in her arms, she knew God had orchestrated this all along. It took many obstacles, tears, and sleepless nights but she would do it again if it meant she could have Isabella.

Journey was sad that Lance wasn't there. Although she shouldn't have been with him, she thought that after everything that happened with Lisa, he deserved to be a part of that moment. She had not spoken to Lance or his parents since the night they picked him up from her apartment, weeks prior.

When Journey had a moment to herself while the baby was sleeping, she decided to text Lance's parents a photo of the baby, saying, "She's here! Meet Isabella!"

Lance's mom, Miss Brenda, called Journey almost immediately.

"Oh, my goodness, Journ! I didn't know you had the baby. How precious!"

"Have you heard from Lance?" Journey asked.

"He is in rehab. He isn't allowed to have a phone, and for the first couple of weeks he was on a strict watch because he threatened to harm himself and was showing signs of depression," Miss Brenda shared.

"Oh that would explain why I haven't heard from him since the night you and Mr. Sam took him away. He hasn't been answering my texts or calls, so I got worried," said Journey.

"Oh yes, dear. We brought him to rehab that night. There were no ifs, ands, or buts. In addition to drinking, he was indulging in cocaine, we later found out. But he can write letters. He has your address. I'm sure he will reach out. Let me know when my husband and I can come to meet our grandbaby! Congrats again, Journ!"

"Y'all can come tomorrow morning; just let me know what time," Journey replied.

"Great! Get some rest; see you tomorrow," Miss Brenda said.

"Bye," Journey whispered as Isabella began tossing and turning in her bassinet.

Journey felt responsible for Lance's freedom being taken away, but she reminded herself that he needed help. He couldn't be around the baby in his current state.

The next morning, Miss Brenda and Mr. Sam were at the hospital bright and early to meet their granddaughter. When they arrived, they came bearing gifts which Journey loved.

They knew Journey had a sweet tooth so they brought her some Reese's Peanut Butter Cups and flowers. Then out of nowhere, Miss Brenda pulled out a huge bag full of clothes and shoes for Isabella.

"Miss Brenda," Journey laughed. "What is all this?"

"You know I had to spoil my first grandbaby. Let me see her."

Journey handed Isabella to Miss Brenda.

Miss Brenda was the life of the party, and Mr. Sam was quiet and sweet. Journey loved Lance's parents because they always showed Journey respect and kindness. Lance's parents were from Barbados, and they had a certain culture that Journey admired. Lance didn't embrace the culture as much as Journey. When Journey and Lance were together she tried to cook Caribbean dishes while Lance usually preferred American food.

Watching Miss Brenda hold Isabella, Journey noticed how much Isabella favored Miss Brenda.

When Journey's forty-eight hours at the hospital were up, Nya and Avery helped her take baby Isabella home.

Weeks went by, and Isabella grew like a weed. Journey took to motherhood quite naturally. She had Isabella on a routine that seemed to work for the both of them.

Things started to get a little cramped in Journey's one-bedroom apartment. She couldn't wait to find a new place. Besides having only minimal space, she didn't like the periodic noise that came from the neighbors upstairs. With a baby, Journey realized the importance of quietness. Isabella was an extremely light sleeper, and if the upstairs neighbors walked too noisily or dropped anything, the sound cascaded down into her apartment and immediately woke Isabella up.

As Journey had gotten older, she wanted a peaceful place—a place that was home to her. Luckily, her best friend was one of the best real estate agents in the city, and Avery was very convincing. Journey had enough for the down payment, but the home prices in the city were skyrocketing, so Journey was hoping Avery would find a flexible seller.

Journey had to meet Avery later that day to look at houses on the east side of town. It would be farther from Journey's job, but she wasn't worried about the commute. She just wanted to get out of her small apartment.

Traveling with a newborn was no small feat, so Journey thought it might be easier if she dropped the baby off with her parents when she went to look at houses. Luckily, many of the houses Avery and Journey were looking at were near her parents' house, so having them watch Isabella would be convenient.

The first house Avery and Journey visited was a farmhouse style home with navy blue shutters on white siding. At first glance, she loved it. When she walked into the house, she was greeted by a beautiful foyer, which led to an equally beautiful living room with a fireplace. The ambiance of the house felt perfect for raising Isabella.

Avery told Journey a little about each seller and their situation. For the first house, Avery said, "The seller is a woman who lost her husband a couple of months ago, and her kids are out of the house, so there is no need for a house of this size. Obviously, she wants the best and highest offer, but this is a private listing, so you are the first to see it. This weekend, there will be an open house."

Journey got scared because she really wanted the house and feared not winning the offer. Avery laughed Journey off because "everyone always loves the first house. Let us look at all the houses first."

"OK, what is the asking price for this house?" Journey asked.

"Asking is $479K. I think it is priced accurately."

"Oh, okay," Journey said, discouraged. Would it help if I wrote a letter to the seller?"

"Yes, that is always a good option. But again, Journ, let's check out all the houses."

"OK," Journey said reluctantly.

They viewed three more houses, but Journey didn't feel the same connection with any of them as she did with the first house. The other three houses were nice, but they didn't seem family friendly. One house had glass everything, and the others had little to no backyard. The first house was perfect. Avery was neutral and encouraged Journey to view one more house that she had arranged to see. On the way to the last house, Avery gave Journey an overview to cheer her up because it was clear Journey was not impressed.

"So, this house is close to your parents' house, about four miles away. It has a small front yard and a decent size backyard. It has three bedrooms, one bath, a beautiful kitchen, and a smaller living room. The sellers are moving out of state and want to close soon."

"OK. Let's see it," Journey replied.

Avery pulled up to the final house, which was located in a cul-de-sac. Journey liked that it was a quiet street. The house was white with a low-pitched red tile roof. It gave a Spanish eclectic vibe, which wasn't what Journey was looking for, but she liked it. When she walked in, to her left was a dining room and to her right was the living room.

Each room was a perfect size. She loved the interior's plain white color. Journey preferred simple; she didn't care for crazy colors.

The kitchen was what sealed the deal for Journey. The kitchen was newly renovated with glazed white marble countertops and light gray stained hardwood floors. The stove looked brand-new; it had stainless steel coating and red knobs. Journey thought to herself: *Nya would love this.*

Avery watched Journey walk through the home with anticipation. She wasn't sure whether Journey liked it because Journey was moving swiftly and quickly through all the rooms: kitchen, living room, bathroom, and then bedrooms.

Journey was very observant. She noticed details the first time and didn't have to spend too long looking at one room.

When Journey met Avery back in the foyer, she inquired about the asking price for that house. Avery said it was going for $455K, which is about the amount Journey had budgeted.

"Why is it cheaper than the first house we saw?" Journey asked.

"Because it is farther from the city. The farther out you go, the cheaper."

For now, Journey wasn't worried about getting to the city. Her job offered great benefits, which enabled her to take three months of maternity leave and use her short-term disability insurance to extend her leave to a full twelve months. Now that Journey was a mother, she wanted to find a job where she had more time to be a mom. She would certainly miss everyone at the firm, but when another door opens, another closes.

Journey loved the last house more than the first one. She pictured the events she would throw there and how she would raise Isabella.

CHAPTER 12

"Out of twenty-eight offers, Journ, your offer was accepted! Your offer wasn't even the highest, but the seller fell in love with your letter. It also helped that you went with their agent's mortgage broker. They felt comfortable with your application because they knew the deal would close using their broker."

When Journey received that call from Avery, she was ecstatic. She was nursing Isabella and had to stop and thank God because that miracle was one God enabled. Journey thought to herself, *Why me? What about the other twenty-seven people? Why me?*

But Journey stopped asking those questions and instead just thanked the Lord.

As soon as she heard the news, Journey began packing up her apartment. Isabella was sleeping, and Journey was on cloud nine. She was grateful and full of happiness.

Journey started packing her closet first. She shuffled through dozens of handbags, birthday cards, and photo albums. For a moment, she got lost in the memories. She read every birthday card she had saved from when she was a young child, and she peered through all the photo albums of her and her family. She teared up. She missed the days of pure innocence when she had been blind to the world and its issues.

Journey packed all those items in a box and emptied her handbags. She once again came across the Bible she had found over a year ago on that devastating day. She immediately opened it. A bookmark was on Romans 8:18: *"For I consider that the sufferings of this present time are not worth comparing with the glory that is to be revealed to us."*

Journey got down on her knees and began thanking God for his glorious and miraculous works. She laid all her worries, fears, and anxieties at Jesus's feet.

Then something wondrous happened. Journey began speaking in other tongues. At that moment, she totally surrendered all, and God had been waiting for her to say yes. She felt a joy she could not explain. Journey continued praising God until Isabella woke from her nap.

Journey couldn't believe that this Bible would be the answer to her many questions. She always wondered why God would allow Lance to do what he did and shatter her heart and trust. But God sometimes allows your heart to be broken so he can mend it. Journey accepted God's plan for her life. Out of excitement, Journey called Zelle to tell him the good news. She wanted to call Zelle because he would understand why this was so pivotal to her. He knew what the walk was like and always prayed for Journey to experience that type of breakthrough.

"Hey, Journ, wassup? How's my beautiful niece?"

"Hey, Zelle. She's good. I'm feeding her now. I have something to tell you," Journey said excitedly.

"What?" Zelle asked eagerly.

"I just got filled with the Holy Spirit," Journey replied as she wept.

"Oh, thank you, Lord! Thank you, Lord!" Zelle yelled. As Zelle's prayers continued, he began speaking in tongues, and Journey joined in.

The sound they shared through that phone was surely a sweet, sweet sound to God's ears. The praise and worship of a brother and sister were wonderful and precious.

Isabella fell asleep in Journey's arms while she and Zelle prayed.

Once the worship stopped, Zelle asked, "How is motherhood going? Have you talked to Lance?"

"No, I haven't. A lot has happened," Journey admitted.

Zelle interrupted, "We don't have to talk about it. That is in the past. Let us move forward."

"You're right. Have you talked to Nya? I feel like I haven't talked to her in weeks."

"That's because you've been in mom mode. I just talked to her last night. She wasn't feeling well, so I brought her some Pho."

Journey placed Isabella in the crib and then put on her AirPods to finish the conversation with Zelle.

"She has probably been working too hard. She needs to rest," Journey said as she straightened up the kitchen.

Being a mother to a newborn caused Journey to forget about how she looked, which had once been a big deal for her. No matter what, she had always looked and felt her best, but the baby had taken most of her time. Additionally, she had a pile of mail on her kitchen counter.

"Why do you feel closer to God now than when we were kids? We used to live at church," Zelle asked.

"To be honest, I think it was because I never got into the Bible. But now it is like the Bible is speaking to me. The Word is the reminder I need each day. Without it, I feel lost."

Zelle chuckled, "I totally understand. That is why we need to read the Word. Praying and worshiping is great, but we can't hear what God is saying without reading His Word."

"Exactly," Journey said while looking at her phone. Avery's name flashed on the screen.

"Hey, Zelle. I'll call you back. Avery is calling."

"OK, Sis. See you on Sunday."

Journey clicked over to the other line. "Hey, Avery. Wassup?"

"Hey, Journ. I just got a call from the seller's agent, and something happened that we didn't catch until we brought in the lawyer to close."

"Oh no. What happened?" Journey asked.

"There is a weird lien on the house. The seller wasn't aware of this, but they are trying to resolve it quickly. It could take up to a year for the bank to clear the lien."

"What?" Journey asked, a tear rolling down her face. I already told my landlord that I was looking for a place and asked if I could end my lease early. I have until September."

"I know, Journ. But it is only the end of June. What do you want to do? Do you want to pull out and look for another place, or do you want to wait?"

"Let me pray on it, and I will let you know," Journey said.

"All right, let me know," Avery replied.

Journey tried to keep her mind off what Avery had told her. She decided to start cleaning the house, starting with the kitchen. Journey sat at the black marble island and opened her mail to shred.

Most of the mail was dumb promotional deals. But Journey saw a square envelope at the bottom. She pulled it from the pile and read the front; the return address was:

Lance Cutler
62 Rose Ln
Vergennes, VT 05491

Vermont. Wow, Miss Brenda was not playing about getting Lance away. Journey eagerly opened the envelope and pulled out the thin sheet of paper inside.

Journey,

I wanted to apologize. I don't think I ever gave you a genuine apology. You have to believe I do love you, Journey.

To think of you with someone else made me sick to my stomach, and there was no way I could be OK with you cheating on me. Although the baby ended up not being mine, I was still unfaithful. It was a stupid mistake. To look at my best friend, my lover, and tell her I cheated. All I felt was shame. Don't think for a second that I did not feel bad about what I had done.

Shame has followed me since that day. From that day on, my life slowly began to crumble. I lost you, I eventually lost my job, I lost my dignity dealing with Lisa, and I lost the opportunity to meet my daughter. My mom told me you had the baby. Isabella, is it? That is a beautiful name.

I also imagine I lost your trust. I never meant to put my hands on you, Journey. It was almost as if each time I did, it wasn't me. My body was being taken over by an angry, jealous, and mean entity. You've known me for a long time; you know I wouldn't hurt a fly.

When my parents came and picked me up from your apartment that night, I felt like a disappointment. Look how far I have fallen. I was a successful financial consultant with a beautiful educated and successful woman. Why would I throw that away?

Finally, I just want to tell you that this wasn't your fault. I still love you, but I know I caused too much damage. I just hope we can at least be friends for Isabella. I can't wait to meet her.

You'll be proud to know that I'm reading my Bible. I've been asking God to guide me through this. I know I have to do this for myself and my family's future.

Lance

Journey started to tear up—not because she was sad, but because that letter felt like the closure she needed. She felt free, and she forgave Lance. Journey continued to pray for his strength, but she could no longer see herself with him, and that was okay.

Suddenly, Journey heard Isabella crying, and she hurried to the bedroom to comfort her. As Journey held Isabella, she began crying. She looked at the tiny human she and Lance had made and was in awe. The crazy thing was that Isabella had Lance's long eyelashes and glistening eyes and Journey's button nose and shiny black hair. God was so clever. Isabella was a perfect mix of Lance and Journey. Journey felt Isabella was God's way of healing and mending her heart. Isabella always smiled at Journey with wide eyes and a beautiful dimple on her left cheek. Journey would melt each time.

Journey felt guilty leaving Isabella with anyone because she believed it was her responsibility as a mother to watch her 24/7. But that day, Journey had the courage to ask her parents to watch Isabella again. She was exhausted and needed a break. Of course, Journey loved spending time with Isabella, but she also wanted to hang out with Avery and Nya.

Journey called Mama Luna, "Hi, Mama."

"Hi, Journ. How is my little grandbaby?"

"She's perfect. I am calling to ask if you would be able to watch Isabella for a few hours. I want to catch up with Nya and Avery," Journey said quickly.

"Of course! We've been waiting to take her. Do you want us to pick her up, or will you drop her off?" Mama Luna asked eagerly.

Journey breathed a sigh of relief. "Um, if you don't mind, it would be really helpful if you could pick her up. Thank you, Ma."

Retired Mama Luna was the best. With so much time on her hands, she loved being needed.

"I know how you are. I'm surprised you even asked," Mama Luna admitted.

"It just feels weird, you know? I don't want to put my responsibilities on anyone else," responded Journey.

"Journey, it takes a village. That is what family is for."

"You're right. I will get Isabella ready. Just let me know when you're downstairs, and I'll buzz you in."

A few hours passed, and Journey heard the buzzer for her apartment.

"Hey, Journey. It's us!"

Journey buzzed her parents in downstairs, and shortly after, they were at Journey's apartment door.

Journey was greeted with big smiles and long hugs. Her parents were so happy to see her.

"Where's Bella?" Mama Luna asked.

"Count on Ma to already have a nickname for Isabella," Journey said with a chuckle.

"You know I couldn't help myself. It just fits her," Mama Luna said, laughing.

"Mm . . . Ma. Let me go get 'Bella,'" Journey mocked.

As Journey brought Isabella out of the bedroom, her parents' faces lit up. Isabella was still asleep, her lashes glistening as she was smiling in her sleep. It was the most precious sight.

Mama Luna sat on the couch, holding Isabella and admiring her while Journey and her dad were catching up in the kitchen.

"Did you find a house you liked, Journ?" her dad asked as he drank his Dunkin Donuts Hazelnut iced coffee.

"Oh, shoot," Journey said with her hand on her forehead. "I'm sorry. There's so much I haven't gotten around to telling y'all. But yes, I did put in an offer on this beautiful house, which is not too far from your house." Journey decided not to concern her parents with the news she just received from Avery.

Journey and her father's conversation was interrupted.

"We should get going, Romero. Journey, you can come to get her in the morning," Mama Luna called from the living room.

"Wait, you're keeping Isabella overnight?" Although Journey could have felt guilty, she was thrilled to get a break. She could finish cleaning the apartment and get her life together.

"Yes. Is that OK?" Mama Luna asked.

"Of course. Let me pack her some extra clothes and diapers."

"No need. We have a room for her with plenty of diapers and clothes."

Journey and her dad shared a look. "Ma, you're too much," Journey said.

"What?" Mama Luna asked, clueless.

"Well, here are a few bags of milk for her," Journey said as she grabbed the breast milk from the freezer.

Journey walked her parents and Isabella to the car. Of course, Mama Luna already had a car seat waiting for Isabella.

Journey loved how much her mom spoiled and loved Isabella. She loved that she could make her mom smile.

On Journey's way back upstairs, she decided to text Avery and Nya in a group chat.

Journey: "Hey! I know it is super last minute, but I am ba-by free until tomorrow. Let's go out to eat and catch up."

Avery: "I'm in. Let's try out that new Italian place downtown. Can I make reservations for five?"

Journey: "Nya?"

Nya: "I don't know. I'm still in bed."

Avery: "Nya, it is almost two in the afternoon."

Journey: "Well, I am not taking no for an answer, so be ready, lol."

Nya: "Fine, I'll be there."

Journey: "Can you pick me up? :)"

Nya: "Ugh, you're annoying. I guess—"

Journey: "You love me. :) See y'all later."

CHAPTER 13

Dinner was quickly approaching, and out of excitement, Journey was ready an hour early. When Nya texted Journey, Journey dashed to the elevator and ran out the front door of her apartment building.

"Hey, Nya," Journey said, hugging Nya from the passenger seat.

Journey got comfortable in her seat and put on her seatbelt. While she was doing so, she felt her phone vibrate. It was a text message from Mama Luna.

"Aww, look at this cute outfit Mom put on, Bella!" Journey showed Nya an image on her phone.

"Bella? We already gave the baby a nickname?"

"You sound like me. Mom started calling her Bella when she picked her up earlier, and it has been on my mind," said Journey.

"Why do we love giving nicknames?" Nya laughed.

Nya headed to the restaurant. It was about a thirty-five-minute ride, and Journey loved being a passenger princess.

Journey had a car but rarely drove it. It was easier to get to work by taking the train. Although Journey was a fantastic driver, she hated driving and always preferred sitting in the passenger seat or the backseat.

During the car ride, Journey and Nya talked about church, and Journey mentioned her eventful morning.

"You know I don't like attention, but I just have to tell you that this morning God filled me with his precious Holy Spirit," Journey said with tears.

Nya also started crying. She knew what that meant. Zelle, Nya, and Journey grew up in the church, and they all knew the value of the Holy Spirit. It was something their grandparents and parents always talked about. For Journey to finally experience the Holy Spirit was something no one could have prepared her for.

"Oh my goodness, Journey, I am so happy for you."

"You're next," Journey teased.

"I know. I feel so left out. Everyone has it but me," Nya whined.

"You gotta surrender everything. I know you like to be in control; I did, too, but the moment I let go, I gave the Holy Spirit a space to dwell."

"I feel like I have been all over the place, and I haven't made the time for God like I used to. I've been going through a lot lately, and I have been hopeless," Nya confessed.

"What's been going on?" Journey asked.

"I don't know. I've been feeling very weak, and most days, I don't even feel like being at the restaurant. You know I usually hate being away."

"Well, you have to take care of yourself, Nya. Your restaurant is in good hands."

"You're right," Nya admitted.

"Let me text Avery and make sure she's there," said Journey.

Journey: "Are you there yet?"

Avery: "Yes! I'm waiting for y'all!"

Journey: "Relax, lol. The reservation isn't until five. It's just now four-thirty."

Avery: "Lol, I'm bored. Hurry up!"

Journey: "We are ten minutes away. Keep our seats warm. :)"

Journey and Nya arrived at the restaurant, and Nya let the valet take her car.

Avery was waiting in one of the booths, her strawberry lemonade almost empty. Journey walked up to the booth and took a seat. "Dang, how long have you been here?"

"Since four-fifteen; they let me sit while I waited for you bean heads."

"Shut up, Avery!" Nya laughed.

Avery motioned to one of the servers. "Do you two know what you want?"

"You know what I am getting: chicken alfredo and a strawberry lemonade," Journey stated.

"Basic," Avery whispered.

Journey shot her a look.

"Yeah, I know what I want," Nya said while holding the menu.

One of the servers arrived, but instead of making eye contact, her head was still in her notepad. She appeared new and nervous. "Good evening. My name is Lisa, and I will be your server today." As the server looked up and saw who she would be serving, her face turned pale. She looked like she had just seen a ghost.

Nya didn't like confrontation, so she avoided eye contact once she realized that it was Lance's Lisa.

"Lisa, Lisa, Lisa," Avery said with a smirk. "We meet again."

"I'll get you a new server. I don't want any issues," Lisa said genuinely.

Journey remained calm. She felt bad for Lisa.

"Please, I need this job. I have a baby to take care of."

"Oh, Lisa, we don't want any trouble either. We would appreciate another server. Thank you," Journey said with a smile.

Lisa scurried off in search of another server.

The table went silent. Avery looked like she was ready to spit on Lisa. She watched as Lisa walked away. Nya's cheeks were red from embarrassment, and Journey had a sympathetic look on her face. Although Lisa did what she did, it hurt Journey to see her like that. Journey and Lisa had once been really good friends, so she was sad to see everything pan out the way it had.

"God don't like ugly. She had been an assistant at a prestigious downtown firm; now she's waiting tables? After all she has done, that is not a coincidence," Avery said.

Thankfully, another server came to cut the silence. He was a tall young man with a glowing tan.

"Sorry about that, ladies. What can I get for you this evening?"

"I'll take the Chicken Alfredo," Journey replied.

"I will have the shrimp scampi with garlic teriyaki salmon," said Avery.

"I'll take the Caesar salad with grilled chicken," Nya said, closing the menu.

"I will put that right in for you ladies. Did you want anything other than water?"

"No, water is fine for now," Journey said.

"Alrighty, I'll bring your food out shortly," the new server said with a smile.

The girls made small talk while they waited for their food. Nya and Avery mostly talked while Journey stared at Lisa navigating through the restaurant.

Avery caught Journey staring at Lisa and quickly spoke. "Hello? Why do you keep looking at her, Journey? That's weird."

"Yeah, I agree with Avery. What's going on?" said Nya.

"Nothing," Journey said; she shrugged their comments off, sat up straight, and focused on Avery sitting across from her.

"Weirdo," blurted Avery with a side eye to Journey.

Journey rolled her eyes and laughed.

After about twenty-five minutes, the server brought the meals to Avery, Nya, and Journey. Everyone dug into their meals except Nya. She stared at her salad and began playing with the lettuce using her fork. Her face twisted in disgust.

Journey asked, "Do you not like it, Ny?"

Before Nya could get a word out, vomit exploded from her mouth right onto the salad. The waiter saw the ordeal from across the restaurant and rushed over.

Patrons at the surrounding tables were looking at Journey's table in confusion.

Avery and Journey looked at each other with concern.

"No worries. I will clean this up and bring you a new salad," the server said.

Nya was utterly embarrassed. "No need. But thank you."

Nya began cleaning her face with a handkerchief and then excused herself from the table to freshen up in the bathroom.

"You thinking what I'm thinking?" Journey asked Avery.

"Mm . . . Nya's definitely pregnant," Avery said matter-of-factly.

When Nya got back to their table, it had been cleaned.

Avery and Journey watched Nya carefully.

When Nya finished patting her face with a handkerchief and sighing, she saw the suspicious looks on Avery's and Journey's faces.

Journey blurted out, "You're pregnant." She said it as a statement, not a question, Journey knew.

"Yes," Nya confirmed.

"What? How did I not know about this? How could you keep this from me? I didn't know you were seeing anyone," Journey said in shock.

"I know, Journ. I didn't mean to keep the pregnancy from you. As far as my relationship, I was trying to see where it was headed," Nya said.

"Well, we see where it headed," Journey said, looking at Nya's stomach. Avery and Nya laughed. Journey continued, "That would explain why you haven't been feeling well. Have you told anyone?"

"No, I wasn't sure what I wanted to do."

Avery said, confused, "What do you mean?"

"I didn't know if I wanted to stay with this person, let alone have a child with him," Nya said.

Journey interjected, "An abortion is out of the question. You always said you would never do that."

"I know . . . I won't . . . , but this is just a lot," Nya said as she yawned.

"I know, Ny. I know," Journey said while reaching in for a hug and rubbing Nya's back. "It is going to be OK. Don't you worry."

Nya started to cry. "It must be the hormones," she said shrugging.

Seeing Nya like that was a sight for sore eyes. Nya was always the strong one who could get through whatever life threw at her, but this time was different; she was vulnerable.

"I never thought I would see the day that Ms. Independent would get married and have a baby," Avery teased.

The conversation was cut short by a phone call. Journey checked her phone, and it was Mama Luna.

"Hey guys, let me take this. Mom is probably just giving me an update on Isabella."

Avery waved Journey off and continued to tease Nya about her mysterious boyfriend, whom they knew nothing about.

Journey answered the phone, "Hi, Ma. How's Bella?" Journey asked.

"Journ, something is not right with Isabella. She is jaundiced, and she is breathing very fast."

Journey tried to remain calm. "Um, Okay. Should we take her to the emergency room?"

The words *emergency room* stopped Avery and Nya's conversation dead in its tracks.

Journey was a new mother; she didn't know how to handle situations like this yet, but she had to make a decision, which was why Mama Luna called her.

"OK, take her to the hospital closest to your house. She should be seen much sooner at that one. I will be there in thirty minutes."

"What happened?" Avery asked.

Journey gathered her purse and opened the Uber app on her phone. "Isabella is jaundiced and breathing very fast. I'm meeting Mom at City Hospital. I'm ordering an Uber now.

"I can take you, Journ," Nya offered.

Journey asked Nya, "You sure you're up to it?"

"Yes, I will be fine. Let's go."

Journey and Nya stormed out of the restaurant.

Avery shouted, "I'll call you later to check in."

The one night I am without her, this happens. I feel so stupid. What kind of mom would leave her newborn to go out to eat?

Nya and Journey arrived at City Hospital's emergency room and didn't see Mama Luna or Isabella. The space was cold and empty, heavy with terrifying energy. Journey then frantically called Mama Luna; the phone rang once, and she answered.

"Hey, Journ. We are in room 5," Mama Luna said.

Journey and Nya ran to room 5 only to see Isabella in worse condition than Mama Luna had described. Isabella's eyes were closed, and rings of purple were around them. Her skin was almost white, and her breathing was very sharp and fast.

Journey ran over to Isabella and couldn't hold back her tears. Mama Luna was in the room alone. Journey asked, "What are they saying?"

"They said it is neonatal sepsis."

Journey asked in panic, "What? What is that?"

Mama Luna stood with her arms crossed as if cold. "The doctor said it is an infection that can trigger an inflammatory response. They started Isabella on an IV drip."

The doctor came into the room and introduced herself to Journey. She extended her hand to greet Journey. "Hello," she said. "You must be the mother. My name is Dr. Ally Pearson."

"Hello," Journey replied tentatively.

The doctor continued, "As I am sure your mother has told you, we gave Isabella an IV to help her fight the infection, but she is not responding to it like we had expected. We would like to admit her, so we can monitor her as she recovers."

"Admit her?" Journeys mouth quivered.

"Yes. I'm afraid that because Isabella is only a few weeks old, her body hasn't developed a strong enough immune system to fight this infection. Her body is weak. I would like to talk about possible options. Do you want a DNR order?"

Journey's life flashed before her eyes. She collapsed in Nya's arms. Mama Luna went to help carry the weight.

The doctor then escorted Isabella out of the room, with her body hooked up to tubes and monitors.

CHAPTER 14

J ourney made it home after spending hours at the hospital with Isabella. Mama Luna and Nya offered to stay at the hospital while Journey went home to shower and pack a bag for Isabella.

She walked in like a zombie, removed her clothes, and hopped into a steaming hot shower. She had to wash the whole night off. It was a long day that started wondrously; Journey had her breakthrough and received the precious Holy Spirit and the news about Nya being pregnant. Journey was in complete awe of the day until she received that phone call from her mother about Isabella.

Journ knew she had to intercede on behalf of Isabella, so she went into deep prayer. She did her best while she was in the shower. Journey prayed as hard and as long as she could. It was around eleven when she got out of the shower and dressed. Then, there was a knock at the door. *Who could have gotten up here without me buzzing them in?*

Journey ran to the door and looked through the peephole. To her utter surprise, it was Joey. *What the . . . ? It's too late for a drop-by.*

She opened the door, and Joey spoke straight away.

"Hi, Journey!" Joey said excitedly. Joey could see the look on Journey's face. On the one hand, she looked confused; on the other, she looked like she had been crying.

"Um . . . , sorry to just pop in, but I wanted to surprise you. I know it is late, but as you know, we had our yearly outing around the corner from here, and I thought I would come to check on you. When I told him we were coworkers, the doorman just let me up, and I didn't know which buzzer to ring."

"I need to talk to that doorman. He can't let just anyone up here," Journey said laughing as she motioned for Joey to enter.

"But how is everything going? Joey paused. Have you been crying?"

"No. Well, yes. I have been praying. When I pray, I tend to cry," said Journey.

Joey dropped his head in awkwardness. "Oh, okay. Where is your baby? I would love to meet her," he said, changing the subject.

When Journey told Joey what had happened with Isabella, she couldn't help but cry because she was so worried.

Journey wept. "I'm so scared that something might happen to my baby."

"That is understandable," Joey said, concerned. "But God did not give us the spirit of fear. We have to trust in Him and trust in His will. He will never leave or forsake you."

Journey was seated on the sofa, and she placed her face in both hands and said, "I know."

Joey stood in front of her but then slowly sat beside Journey and gently touched her leg. It was the reassurance Journey needed to keep her head up.

"Listen, you should come to church with me tomorrow. A pastor is visiting from California. She is supposed to be very motivational. Maybe it would be good for you."

Journey rubbed her arm in thought, "I don't know. I should be at the hospital with Isabella."

Joey made eye contact with Journey's sad eyes; "We can go right after church. I think going would be good for you."

Journey hesitated but eventually agreed to go. She quickly changed the subject, "I meant to ask you the last time I saw you: How is everything with Carla? Are you OK now that the divorce is finalized?"

A smirk appeared on Joey's face. "Let's just say that I am so glad I got out of that crazy family. I should have known it wasn't going to work out. Carla didn't believe in God, and she hated when I would ask her to come to church with me. That never sat well with my soul, but I thought praying about it would make her eventually come. But that never happened. I guess that wasn't the path for us."

Journey's phone rang. She shut the ringer off and continued her conversation. Journey didn't want to be rude. Her phone rang again. For a moment, Journey completely forgot about her circumstances and was, at the moment, enjoying a decent conversation with a decent human. Journey was brought back to reality when she saw her mother's name on her phone.

"Excuse me, Joey; it's my mom. It could be about Isabella," Journey said, walking away to take the phone call in her bedroom.

"Of course," Joey said while sitting on the sofa in the living room.

"Hey, Ma. How is everything? I am about to leave soon."

"The doctor wants you to come back. Isabella stopped breathing, and they had to give her rescue breaths."

Journey dropped her phone and couldn't move for a moment.

Joey heard the noise and asked, "Are you okay, Journey?" When he didn't hear back from her, he ran to her bedroom and knocked on the door before entering.

"Hey," he said cautiously, pushing the door open. He saw Journey flash a sad look; then she said, "I have to go back to the hospital."

"OK, I will take you there. Let's go."

Journey and Joey stormed out of Journey's apartment as quickly as possible. Joey wasted no time getting to the hospital. He sped through streetlights and stop signs. He could tell by the look on Journey's face that she was worried. Joey wanted to help in any way he could.

After a forty-five-minute ride turned into a twenty-five-minute drive, Joey stopped at the hospital's main entrance. Journey raced from the car to the hospital floor where Isabella was. As usual, the hospital smelled like latex, and the atmosphere was cold. Journey hated hospitals. When she got to the fifth floor, she became nauseated. She was overwhelmed with emotions and didn't know how to regulate them.

Mama Luna caught Journey in the hallway and noticed that she looked pale.

"What's wrong, Journ?" her mother asked.

"Nothing, nothing. Where's Isabella?" Journey fought through the exhaustion.

"She's in the room. The doctors are in there taking her vitals again," Mama Luna said, looking right into Journey's eyes, searching for an answer.

Mama Luna wrapped her right arm around Journey's left arm and walked her the few steps into Isabella's room.

As Journey entered the room and saw that all the color had drained from Isabella's face, she dropped to her knees. Nya was out grabbing something to eat, and Mama Luna watched as her daughter and granddaughter lay helpless.

Suddenly, Journey felt someone touch her shoulder. It was Joey. Journey tried to speak, but Joey shook his head and said, "Pray. Touch your daughter and pray for her."

When Nya returned to the room, she saw hands being held and worship being lifted. She didn't say anything, so she joined hands with Mama Luna and prayed. The atmosphere was thick with God's peace. After twenty-five minutes of diligently praying over Isabella, everyone felt and looked lighter. Journey looked well-rested and, most of all, hopeful.

"Thank you for that, Joey," Journey said as she wiped her eyes. Mama Luna and Nya just peered at Journey and looked at Joey.

"Oh, I'm sorry. Joey, this is my mom, Luna, and my sister Nya. Joey is a friend from work; we have been colleagues for a few years."

Joey exchanged handshakes with Nya and Mama Luna, "But I will leave you to it. I just wanted to make sure you and Isabella were OK."

"Thank you, Joey. I appreciate it. I will see you at church tomorrow," Journey said with a smile.

"Oh, I didn't expect you to go after what happened today. But you know what? I am glad you are, and I'm sure God will be too." Joey returned her smile. He waved goodbye to everyone in the room and disappeared into the chaos of the hallway.

"You should go home and get some rest. A hospital isn't the best place for a pregnant woman," Mama Luna advised as she kissed Nya.

Then, Journey gave Nya a hug and a kiss on the cheek, "Get home safe."

Once Nya was gone, Journey looked at her mother curiously. "You knew Ny was pregnant?"

"Of course, I did. A mother always knows. I knew before she did," Mama Luna said.

"Wow," Journey said in disbelief. "Here I was thinking Nya had left me out. I only found out because she was throwing up at dinner."

Shoot, I forgot to text Avery to let her know how Isabella is doing.

"One second, Mom, I have to call Avery." Journey searched her coat pocket and purse for her phone.

Mama Luna quickly interrupted, saying "Well, I am going to head out. Dad is around the corner. He wasn't up to being in the same hospital where Uncle Ernie died, so he just dropped me off. You should have seen him, Journ; he was a mess. I was a mess internally, but you know I can keep it together for everyone's sake. I had to calm him down the whole car ride to the emergency room," Mama Luna said as her hand shot up for extra emphasis.

Journey chuckled softly and said, "Yeah, I know how Dad is. Would you mind if I caught a ride back with you all?"

"You sure? I assumed you would stay the night here."

"No. Staying here will just make me worry. I put it in God's hands. I will come to see her tomorrow after church."

"OK, sure," Mama Luna said as she led the way out of the room—but not until after giving Isabella one more glance.

Mama Luna looked back to make sure Journey was not too far behind. She caught Journey standing in front of Isabella's crib, smiling. Mama Luna wasn't sure if it was a peaceful smile or hurt underneath the smile, but she didn't pry. She waited patiently until Journey was ready.

When Journey got home, she was starving. She had been fasting without noticing as her mind was focused on a miracle for Isabella and interceding on Isabella's behalf. Although it wasn't an intentional sacrifice, she felt God was pleased with her dedication and faith in a breakthrough. Journey put her phone on the charger and promptly fell asleep.

The next morning, as promised, Journey was ready to go to Joey's church. She texted Joey asking for the address and met him there. The church was not that big; it was a small brick building on the corner of a quiet street.

Joey spotted Journey as she walked into the service and waved her down to catch her attention. Journey walked in slowly and sat next to Joey.

"Glad you came. You're right on time. Service is about to begin," Joey explained.

Journey gave Joey a gentle smile.

After several performances from the praise team, which consisted of four young women singing worship music, the preacher came to the pulpit. She began praying and then got into the Word. Her topic that day was the "Suffering of the Righteous." She explained the story of Job and highlighted that suffering is to be expected in a world of sin. Because God allows us free will, He won't altogether prevent us going through hardships.

When the preacher was wrapping up, she made an altar call that asked anyone desiring prayer to come to the front. Many church members quickly formed a line from the front of the altar all the way to the back of the church. When Journey arrived at the front of the prayer line, it was her turn for prayer. The pastor embraced Journey's face with both hands and smiled at Journey. She said, "I saw you when you walked in. God is pleased to see you in the house of the Lord. The Holy Spirit told me to tell you this message: 'Your daughter is healed.' I don't know your situation, but the Lord told me to tell you that your gift of healing has delivered your daughter from a life-threatening illness. The doctors won't know what happened. Praise him in advance."

The preacher walked away and left Journey to lift her hands to the Lord in total surrender and hope. Whether Journey fully believed it or not, she wanted to. She had to.

CHAPTER 15

After Journey visited Joey's church, Isabella got better each day. Although Isabella was still in the hospital, Journey continued to remain hopeful. Joey and Journey's relationship had grown, too. Joey was a comfort during the hard times. He brought Journey even closer to God. It had been exactly seven days since Isabella stopped breathing. Each day after, she continued to improve.

The doctors said that Journey would probably be able to bring Isabella home in a couple of days. Over the past week, Journey's faith and trust in God had grown more than ever. She always thanked God for the blessings in her life, and she repeated the same prayers every night. In the past, when things didn't go Journey's way, she often questioned God. Sometimes, she would stop hoping and praying altogether. She had a conditional relationship with God. She would continue to pray as long as he was doing stuff for her. But that is not how it is supposed to be at all. God is merciful and gracious but also knows how to make a point.

Journey could have easily resorted to her old ways and questioned God's purpose for Isabella getting sick so soon after birth. But God had instilled in her a glorious gift through Isabella's illness. Had Journey not turned to prayer in her time of need, she may not have seen the miracle God intended.

As people who believe in God, we often think that everything should be sunshine and rainbows. Even Jesus Himself went through an unspeakable tragedy. Are we better than Him? While we are on this earth, we must endure suffering, but the silver lining is that God will never leave or forsake us. Solace and victory are always on the other side of the battle; but we must have faith and trust that God can and will see us through our storms.

Joey dropped Journey off at her apartment after another church service. Journey finally had time to catch her breath as she sat alone and took in her surroundings. She suddenly realized that she had been so busy with her personal life that she had forgotten to get back to Avery about the house. It was time to give Avery a call.

"Hey, Avery, I'm sorry I haven't gotten back to you about Isabella or the house, but everything has been so hectic. I have been trying to keep myself in good spirits and focus on one thing at a time."

"I understand. How is Isabella? Nya has been keeping me updated between her morning sickness episodes."

Journey laughed and said, "Isabella is progressing well. As for Nya . . . I still cannot believe she's pregnant."

"And has a boyfriend," Avery added.

"Girl, that is a whole other story. When Isabella leaves the hospital, we will have to revisit that conversation."

"For sure, for sure. So, I wanted to talk to you about the offer and the house situation."

"Yeah. I was just thinking about that. After praying and fasting, we should keep the offer in place. God will supply. Sorry, it took me so long to get back to you."

"No worries. I already told the seller's agent that you would hang on," Avery said with a chuckle.

Journey pretended to be shocked, "What? You didn't even know what I was going to decide."

Avery called her bluff. "Girl, I know you."

"But let me call you later. Someone is at the door," Journey yelled.

"OK, but don't forget. It's important."

* * * * * *

Journey ran to the door; she already knew who it was. She noticed Joey had left his Bible and was sure he would be back for it.

Journey opened the door, Bible in hand. As she swung open the door, she said playfully, "I knew you would be back for your favorite Bible."

And there he was: Lance. Looking finer than ever, Journey thought. He had his head down when Journey opened the door; he appeared to be nervous. He was wearing a clean gray Nike sweatshirt with matching shorts and white sneakers. His hair was freshly cut, and his curls were big and shiny. He smelled amazing.

Journey almost forgot that he was the father of her child.

She pushed back this newfound distraction and asked God to keep her strong. Journey and Lance have been through a lot, but sometimes, all you can do is remember the good and fun times. That is what Journey was thinking about at that moment.

"Hey, Lance. You look good."

"Thanks, Journ. Can I come in?" Lance asked uncomfortably.

Journey watched Lance walk past her and sit down on the couch. She locked the door and headed his way. "What's going on, Lance?"

"I just got out of rehab a couple of days ago and wanted to clean myself up before meeting Isabella."

"Um. Well, I am glad you are better. You seem much better. But Isabella is not here right now."

"Yeah, I know. Mama Luna told my parents that she was in the hospital, and I came here to talk to you."

"About what?"

"I want to be in Isabella's life. I know I have messed up a lot lately, and I am ready to earn your trust back and meet Isabella whenever you feel is best."

"Well, I really appreciate that. You know me. I would never keep you from your child. Because this is all new to you, I will, of course, be there when you visit."

"Oh yeah, there is another thing. I don't have any place to go."

Journey was confused as to why he was bringing that issue up to her. "Your parents?" Journey asked.

"I can't stay with them. I was hoping I could stay with you. I wouldn't ask if I wasn't desperate."

"I don't know, Lance. That is a lot to ask. I don't think that is a good idea."

"Understandable. Didn't hurt to ask," Lance said and shrugged.

"Where are you staying right now?" Journey asked.

"I've been staying at a hotel. But I can't afford to stay too long without a job," explained Lance.

Journey said, "I can ask Avery if she can help you find a place you can afford. I have to call her anyway. Also, I have a few friends in the financial district that may be able to help you with a job," Journey offered.

"Yes, I would appreciate that. I need a fresh start. I am clean now, and I don't want to go back. I have enough saved to cover rent for a few months." Lance took a pen out of his pocket and grabbed a piece of paper from the table in front of the couch. "Here is my new number. Feel free to text me whenever. I would love to meet Isabella when you're ready. You can give Avery my number too if she'd rather speak to me directly."

"OK. Will do," Journey said, nodding her head.

"I will always love you, Journey," Lance said as he kissed her cheek and walked out the door into the hallway.

When Journey closed the door, she melted on the floor. She realized she still loved Lance and wanted to hug his slim body so tightly. He wore that same cologne that she loved when they were together. But he also looked so vulnerable and in need. That was Journey's weakness. No matter what a person did to Journey, she would push her feelings aside and assist them when they were in need. Her heart was too big for most. But she thanked God every day for a heart like that. As Journey got older, she realized how evil some individuals could be and how people can take advantage of someone with a good heart.

Being sacrificially kind never served Journey well. Although she wanted to help Lance, she knew she had to support herself first.

After Lance left, Journey called Avery back, and she answered on the last ring.

"Journ?"

"Hey, yeah I'm here," Journey said.

"I spoke with the seller's agent earlier and learned that the sellers have paid to clear the lien off the house. We are all set to close!

"Oh, thank goodness! I needed good news today."

"Thank you for trusting me to find you your dream house!"

"Of course! Oh yeah, Lance is looking for a place—something affordable. He is currently looking for a job, not sure how that works," Journey said.

"Hmm, typically landlords want recent paystubs to prove that prospective tenants can afford the rent. If someone is unemployed, they aren't a strong candidate."

"What would help even though he doesn't have a job right now?"

"A cosigner would help. I have a list of landlords that I work with often that would trust my word if I brought them a client. Can I trust Lance? I am only considering this because of you, not because of him."

"I know, Avery; I appreciate it. But you can trust me," Journey said. "If I cosign for him, would that help move things forward?"

"It would, but I wouldn't recommend you do that if you don't want to get burned if he misses a payment."

"I know what's at stake. I want to help him. He has enough money to cover the move-in costs, and hopefully he'll find a job."

"Alrighty, I will make some calls," Avery promised.

CHAPTER 16

*Z*elle called Journey bright and early.

"Hello," Journey said with her eyes still closed.

"Hi, Journ. Do you plan on coming to the hospital this morning?"

Journey rubbed her eyes and sat up in bed, "Why? What time is it?"

"It's 7:15 a.m.," Zelle stated.

"Why are you calling so early?" Journey asked.

"I'll just cut to the chase. I'm checking to see if you will be coming to the hospital to see Isabella because Nya was admitted to the ICU a couple of hours ago. Did you know she was pregnant? I just met her boyfriend."

That got Journey on her feet with her eyes wide open. "Wa . . . wait . . . what? What is wrong with Nya? Boyfriend? What is going on?"

"Hmm, we are not exactly sure. The doctors are running tests, but I guess she was experiencing some ovarian pain and having back spasms. Donny said she eventually passed out, and that's when he brought her to the hospital."

"Who the heck is Donny?" Journey asked, confused.

"Oh, sorry. That's Nya's boyfriend's name," Zelle said matter-of-factly.

"Gosh, I pray she's not miscarrying. Let me get ready, and I will be right over."

As much as Journey wanted to feel sorry for Nya and cry, she couldn't. Journey was in go mode. She dressed quickly, grabbed her keys, and rushed out of her apartment.

On the way to the hospital, Journey called Zelle back and initiated prayer. In her own journey, she always meditated on 1 Thessalonians 5:17, which says, "*Pray without ceasing.*" That is what she and Zelle did until Journey arrived at the hospital. Journey didn't have time to look for the garage and park, so she allowed the valet to take care of her car. Before hanging up the phone, Journey asked for Nya's floor and room number. Zelle was waiting in the lobby, and they walked up to the room together.

Although visiting hours had not yet started, the doctors made an exception considering the severity of Nya's case.

When Journey arrived in Nya's room, peace flooded her heart, which was weird considering that Nya had IVs in both arms. Nya's eyes were closed, but they were black on the outside, and her skin was scaly and pale. Although Zelle, Donny, and Journey's parents were in the room, when Journey stood there staring at Nya, she felt like she was the only person in the room.

Journey didn't greet anyone; she just walked over to Nya and placed a hand on her cold face and declared, "In the name of Jesus, Nya, you are healed." Journey smiled and moved some of Nya's curly locks out of her face.

Journey then turned around to greet everyone. Nya's boyfriend was not what Journey expected at all. Nya was a simple lady who worked very hard. She never seemed to care to maintain a relationship, especially with someone who wanted to take her independence from her. But Donny seemed different. He had the kindest eyes, brown skin, and dimples that sank deep into his cheeks. He towered over Zelle, who was six feet three, and his smile lit up the room. Journey always thought if Nya ever got a boyfriend, he would be a boring but cute man. Donny looked anything but boring; he looked like an exciting person and full of adventure. Journey could not help but be happy about that.

"Hi, I'm Donny, Nya's boyfriend. Nice to meet you."

"Hi Donny, I'm Nya's sister Journey."

"Oh yes, I hear a lot about you. Nya loves you."

Journey snickered and glanced toward Nya's body on the hospital bed. "Yeah, I love her too," she said. "How did you two meet?"

"Well, we ran into each other at church," Donny answered.

Journey and Zelle shared a suspicious and confused glance.

"Church?" Journey asked as if she hadn't heard correctly the first time.

"Yes. First Baptist on Twenty-Third Street."

"Interesting," Journey said as she shot a look at the sleeping Nya.

Not soon after, the doctors came in to update the family on what was happening with Nya. The doctor was a tall black woman with gray wavy coils and a huge smile that revealed a gap in the middle of her otherwise perfect teeth.

It was almost as if Nya knew the doctor was in the room because after the doctor greeted everyone, Nya woke up.

"Hi, Nya," the doctor said sweetly. "How are you feeling?"

"Exhausted," responded Nya.

The doctor shot Nya a sympathetic look and continued. "It looks like you have cysts on both ovaries. Based on your pregnancy and the size of these cysts, it is no wonder that your symptoms have been unbearable. Cysts this size can cause numbness and muscle spasms. We will have to remove your ovaries."

"Never thought I could be a mother anyway," Nya said flatly.

"Nya, don't say stuff like that. You're going to be a great mom, and this baby will be healthy," Journey snapped.

The doctor interrupted. "We won't operate until after you have given birth. My only worry is that the pressure on your ovaries throughout your pregnancy and waiting to operate may cause the cysts to rupture, and that could be fatal."

"So, what do you suggest?" Journey asked the doctor.

"All we can do is wait and pray—wait to see how the symptoms affect Nya. In the meantime, Tylenol and heating pads may help manage the pain and reduce the chance of added inflammation."

"Thank you, doctor," Journey said as the doctor left the room.

Journey turned to Zelle, "What is going on? Our family can't seem to catch a break."

"It may appear that way, but I am sure God will bring us through," Zelle assured her.

"Yeah, you have to be right. I am going to check on Isabella," Journey said.

"I'll come with you," Zelle insisted.

When Zelle and Journey arrived on the floor where Isabella was, Journey's face lit up. The nurse was holding Isabella, and Isabella smiled. She looked so happy. A tear rolled down Journey's face in complete gratitude. She said to herself, "Thank God," because it was God who had healed Isabella. She looked amazing.

Zelle reached out to take Isabella from the nurse. She was sleeping but knew she was in the arms of someone who loved her.

A nurse saw Journey enter the room and ran to her excitedly and said, "Hi, Journey. We just called you!"

"Oh? For what?" Journey asked.

"We called to inform you that Isabella's vitals have been consistent. She's much stronger now, and she is ready to be discharged later this afternoon."

"Oh, my goodness! That is great news," responded Journey.

Meanwhile, Zelle sang happily to Isabella while rocking her in his arms.

Journey started getting emotional but told the nurse, "Thank you."

"I know you've been through a lot. It has been a long journey, but you kept your faith and now look." The nurse continued, "I will let you and your brother spend some time with her. After that, come to the nurses' station to complete the discharge paperwork."

"Sounds good. Thank you," Journey said gratefully.

Before Journey left the hospital with Isabella, she checked on Nya. Everyone else had left. It was just Journey and a sleeping Nya. Journey stared at Nya in awe of how strong she was. Journey knew Nya would survive this, and she believed that Nya was meant to be a mother. There was nothing Nya could not do. She had looked up to Nya her whole life, and this was the first time Journey had seen Nya so vulnerable; it broke her heart. But rather than sulk and cry about Nya's condition, Journey believed everything would be fine. Nya would recover and carry a healthy baby to full term.

When Journey finally arrived home with Isabella, she was so excited. Journey thought it best to call Lance over to the apartment. They have been in contact for the last few days, and Journey has been updating Lance on Isabella's progress. She texted, "Hey, Lance, I just brought Isabella home from the hospital. Feel free to come by and meet her."

Instead of responding to Journey's text message, Lance decided to give her a call. When Journey answered on the first ring, he said, "Hey, Journey. Should I bring anything? I am so nervous but so excited at the same time."

"No, you're good," Journey giggled. "I have everything here."

"OK . . . OK. I'm on my way!"

"OK. Let me know when you're downstairs."

Journey hung up the phone and went to check on Isabella. Before Lance showed up, she decided to call her dad to check on Nya.

Dad answered on the first ring. "Hey, honey. How's Bella?"

"She's good. She is napping right now. But I am calling to see how Nya is doing."

"Hold on, baby. The doctor is talking to Nya right now."

Journey listened in and overheard the conversation. The doctor was recommending that Nya seek counseling. She has been through a lot of trauma with this ordeal, and the doctor thought it best for Nya to seek such help. Nya seemed receptive.

Then Journey heard Mama Luna interrupt, "Oh no. Christians don't believe in counseling. We will put our trust in the Lord."

Journey could feel the awkwardness over the phone.

"Ya . . . Journey, I will call you back. Nya and your mom are fussin'."

Journey was so annoyed with her mother's comment. Especially since she believed that therapy had helped her expose some of the things she had been facing, which enabled her to take the matter to God. Proverbs 13:10 states, *"By insolence comes nothing but strife, but with those who take advice is wisdom."*

How could my mom be so short-sighted? She's never gone through what Nya is going through.

Journey heard a knock at the door. She had forgotten Lance used to live in the building and that he was close to the doormen. She knew it was him.

When she opened the door, she saw Lance's moisturized black curls and wide smile. He looked genuinely happy, much better than the last time she saw him. He was holding flowers. Journey smiled.

"Hi, Journey," Lance said as he placed a peck on Journey's cheek.

"Hey, Lance. Flowers aren't a good gift to give a baby," Journey said with a smirk.

"Oh, yeah, I know. They're for you. Thank you for putting in a good word at that brokerage firm downtown. I got the job on the spot! They loved me. Avery and I found the perfect apartment, not too far from my job. Everything has been going well lately," Lance said as he gave Journey the daisies he was holding.

"Aww, you are so welcome! I am so happy for you! Now I won't need to cosign," Journey said with a genuine smile. "Let me get Isabella; she's in the bedroom taking a nap."

Journey woke Isabella up and brought her to the living room couch. She sat beside a nervous yet excited Lance and placed Isabella in his arms.

Isabella's eyes met Lance's. The two shared a moment, and Journey saw a smile from Isabella and a tear from Lance.

"I just met Isabella, but I never thought I could love someone so much," Lance said. "I can't believe I treated you as I did when this angel was in your belly," he said as he began to cry.

Journey had hoped he wouldn't bring that up. She was trying to move on from that dark time in her life. But Journey tried to be strong and offered encouraging words as she noticed Lance needed them.

"She's a part of you," Journey said, smiling. "I would do anything for that girl."

Without taking his eyes off Isabella, Lance nodded in agreement. For the next thirty or so minutes, Journey soaked it all in. Watching Isabella fall asleep on Lance's chest was magical.

Journey took the opportunity to continue packing up the house. Although it wasn't confirmed how soon she could move into her new house, she trusted God and decided to continue packing as a way showing faith. Not too long after Journey began packing boxes with plates and silverware, Lance asked a question.

"Where do you want me to put her? I can help you pack up."

"Oh, thanks. You can put her in the bassinet in the bedroom," Journey instructed.

Lance very carefully carried Isabella to the bedroom and placed her safely in the bassinet, with Journey's help and guidance.

"What do you need help with?"

Journey looked around the kitchen momentarily and said, "You can continue clearing out the cabinets. I want to clean them."

Lance began removing the dishes from the cabinet. He occasionally stole glances at Journey while she packed Tupperware in a small cardboard box. At one point, Journey turned around and caught Lance staring at her.

"What?" Journey asked, blushing.

"How could I have been so stupid?" Lance wondered out loud.

Journey couldn't hold back. Finally, she felt it was time to express the pain he caused her. "Well, I'm not going to lie. You hurt me beyond words, from the infidelity to putting your hands on me. I never in a million years thought you would treat me like that. In a way, I resented you for that. I loved you, Lance. I loved you hard and unconditionally."

Lance rushed over to Journey as soon as tears began to fall down her face. He grabbed her face and acknowledged, "I know, Journ. I never meant to hurt you. That was all me. I wasn't well; I was unhinged. Please don't blame yourself for my behavior; I have no excuse." Lance began to tear up as well.

The two hugged each other tightly. It was a healing hug for them both. When Lance wrapped his arms around Journey, she smiled inside. It felt like their very first hug. She loved that man.

When Lance broke away from the hug, he and Journey locked eyes. Lance looked at Journey's lips. His hunger for her lips was quickly and intimately fed.

CHAPTER 17

J ourney visited Nya at the hospital almost daily. Nya had been there for what seemed like forever, though it had only been weeks. She and Journey began having deep conversations, and Journey saw a side of Nya she had never known.

"To be honest, Journey. I always opted to be alone because I never thought anyone would love me. I never imagined someone being patient with me and loving me. What do I have to offer? I made my business my life because I thought I was a liability. I become a different person in a relationship; I feel too deeply, and I feared that my feelings would never be reciprocated. Donny is different. He is amazing, but what am I?" Nya continued. "When I found out I was pregnant, I was ecstatic because I could have a piece of me to love forever, but I couldn't show my happiness because I had been let down every time I got my hopes up. Why do I deserve this?"

"Why don't you deserve this, Ny?" Journey asked.

Nya said, "When Uncle Ernie did what he did to me and to you, I became angry with God. Mom and Dad were faithful Christians; how could that happen to us—God's children? I eventually forgave Uncle Ernie and repented for my lapse in judgment and my anger toward God. But that situation took a huge spiritual toll on me. Even after all those years, I still felt guilty; I believed I had to accept that my fate was to be single and childless for the rest of my life."

Journey replied, "That's not how God works, Ny. He isn't going to hold things against us. When we repent, we are forgiven. Jesus paid the price, so we have that option. Don't you dare let the enemy take the blessings God has given you."

Nya began crying uncontrollably. Journey quickly embraced Nya and let her tears fall on her shirt. Her big sister needed her, and for once, it was time for Nya to be held.

Nya and Journey sat in silence until Nya broke the silence.

Nya stared at the bare hospital wall. "You're right, Journey. I'm not going to lie; it will take some time for me to feel fully deserving, but you are absolutely right. This baby is a blessing. Donny is a blessing. Everything I have acquired has been by the grace of God, and I am eternally grateful."

After two weeks in the hospital, Nya was good enough to go home. Donny was by her side the entire time. Journey loved that Nya had someone to love. Love was a wonderful experience, especially when it was pure and genuine.

Before Nya was discharged, the doctors told her that when she came into the hospital, the cyst on her left ovary was six centimeters, and the one on her right ovary was thirteen centimeters.

Nya's doctor said, "It is a miracle you were able to conceive. However, we are not sure your pregnancy will continue to full term. We cannot predict how big the cysts will get. Like we said when you first arrived, the cysts can rupture."

Nya didn't know how to take the news because she was too exhausted. Although she had been in the hospital for two weeks, she hadn't gotten much rest. The food was not what she was used to, and the bed was extremely uncomfortable. She couldn't wait to go home. Nya was also spiritually exhausted. She started praying quite often while in the hospital, and because she was weak, she surrendered everything to God: her worries, her health, and her future.

Journey had fasted the entire time that Nya was in the hospital. She was determined to see a breakthrough in Nya's case. When Journey visited Nya in the hospital, she would place her hand over Nya's stomach and pray for a miracle—for the cysts to go away and for Nya's baby to be healthy and a light to this world. Journey understood that there must be a reason we go through what we go through, even if we never get the answer. She believed that trusting in God brings the reassurance and peace we desire.

The doctor quickly left the room to handle Nya's discharge. The atmosphere felt heavy, so Nya broke the silence once again.

"What's going on with you? What's new?" Nya asked.

Journey choked. Her caramel face turned pale. She never wanted to admit her faults to Nya, who never judged, but disappointment pierced Journey.

Nya continued, "I know something is up. I can feel it. You've been weird the last couple of times you visited."

"Yeah . . . well. Lance came by to meet Isabella," Journey admitted.

"Oh no, Journey, please tell me you didn't," Nya said with a suspicious look.

"It was just a kiss, nothing more," muttered Journey.

"Journey. That is enough. That is all it takes," Nya observed.

"I know, Ny. Trust me. I already beat myself up about it," Journey paused. Then she continued, "It's weird. Months ago, I would have loved to work things out with Lance. The feeling was mutual when the kiss happened, but I saw how he looked at me. I knew he thought there was still a chance, but the kiss showed me that I don't feel the same way. Of course I felt guilty for leading him on and being disobedient to God. He already showed me who Lance was, and that guilt reminded me of what God had brought me through. Some things are best left in the past."

"Have y'all talked since?" Nya asked.

"I haven't responded to any of his text messages because I don't know what to say."

"Journey!" Nya with an understanding smile.

Nya's doctor interrupted their conversation.

"Nya, here is your paperwork. Check out at the front desk, and you should be all set. It has been a pleasure."

"Thank you, Dr. Jones. I cannot wait to take a real shower and get some real food," Nya said, arms stretched above her head and a smile on her face.

"I bet," Dr. Jones agreed. "I will certainly miss having you as my patient, but I am thrilled to know you are well enough to go home."

"Right back at cha, Dr. Jones. I feel like you were "God-sent." Literally. From sharing Scriptures with me daily to uplifting my spirit, you have been a blessing to me. You truly are a God-fearing woman."

Dr. Jones placed a hand on her chest and smiled as she said, "Thank you for those kind words, Nya."

Nya had one last request: "Actually, before I go, can we check my stomach one last time? For . . . the baby?" Journey knew that wasn't what Nya was concerned about. She was interested in the cysts.

"Sure, I don't see why not," Dr. Jones said.

Dr. Jones sat in front of the monitor and applied the cold gel to Nya's protruding stomach. "Okay. So here's the baby. Let's scroll down to locate the cysts. Hmm, that's strange."

"What do you see, Dr. Jones?" Nya asked, worried.

"I don't see anything; that's the problem. Let me call in a colleague for a second opinion," Dr. Jones said, confused.

CHAPTER 18

Months after Journey moved into her new house, she fell into a deep depression in the weeks leading up to the end of her maternity leave. She was stressed about leaving her baby and going back to work. Being a lawyer was not as important to her now that she was a mom. It was impossible for Journey to wrap her head around the fact that something she had worked her whole life for and put her all into was now something she no longer desired. She feared that her transition into motherhood and sweet bliss was ending.

"Avery, I need you," Journey texted her best friend.

Avery: "Girl, yes! Nya told me about your little escapade with Lance!"

Journey: "Ugh. Dang Nya. Always telling my business, lol. I need to vent! Come over!"

Avery: "All right, all right. I'll be over soon. I'm honestly just coming over to see my god baby."

Journey: "Yeah, yeah. Bring some snacks, why don't ya!"

Avery: "You got it!"

While Journey waited for Avery to come over, she searched the internet for other suitable careers or a job that would allow her more time with Isabella. But the jobs she found didn't pay nearly enough or didn't interest her. Journey looked into the private sector, education, and the financial district. Nothing caught her eye.

Being a lawyer was about defending people, and she once loved it. But as she looked in the mirror and reminisced about everything she had been through, she realized that she had never defended herself. That disgusted her. She no longer had a desire to defend people in that profession any longer. She didn't want to deal with the stress of being a lawyer anymore; that realization devastated her because she had worked her whole career to get where she was in life.

But being a mother had directed her into new perspectives and a different mindset. Unfortunately, Journey did not have the luxury of not working. She had a mortgage and an infant; she needed to figure something out. But the more she looked for careers, the more discouraged she felt. What jobs could lawyers do other than being lawyers?

Journey's thoughts were interrupted by a notification from her ring camera. Someone was at the door. Avery had finally arrived, and she was holding a bag full of candy and drinks.

Avery and Journey talked for hours between the Reese's Peanut Butter Cups and numerous throwback movies playing in the shadows of their conversation. Journey was grateful Isabella was on a consistent sleep schedule, which meant she slept through the night. Journey never thought she would get past the sleepless nights Isabella used to trigger when she was a newborn.

"I didn't realize how much I needed this, Avery. I feel so numb."

Avery asked in a concerned tone, "What do you mean numb? Do you think you are depressed?"

"No, no. Nothing like that. I just don't have passion or ambition like I used to. I guess I am searching for contentment, so I think it's hard to find another job that is right for me now."

"I totally get it. The good thing is that you have a job to return to until you figure it out." Avery suggested.

"Yeah, I guess you're right."

"Have you been attending church and keeping up with reading the Word?"

"Ugh, no, I have been reading the Scripture of the day in a devotional and praying, but I feel like I have a mind block. I can't get deep into my praying like I used to. On top of being exhausted from being a single mother, my mind is also sleep-deprived. I have not been going to church because I have been sleeping in, but I believe going to church would get my mind off everything that is weighing me down. After having Isabella, my hormones have been all over the place, so I have been feeling resentful toward Lance for how he treated me while I was pregnant, for cheating on me, and for the simple fact he can pick and choose when he wants to be a parent while I don't have that option. I have to be a 24/7 parent, and although it has been the best experience of my life, it is exhausting to be alone."

"Journ, I see how you are when you are 100 percent for God, reading your Bible, praying, and attending church. It affects you if you are not doing those things."

"I hate to be mean, but can I be frank?" asked Journey.

"Of course; it is me, Journ. You can tell me anything, no judgments."

Journey admitted, "I love that Lance comes over every weekend to help, but when he comes over, it's a lot. He asks for my help to feed her and to change her diaper. I technically don't have a moment to step away without being called back. He can drop the responsibility and use the bathroom or make a store run without permission, and I can't. It feels like more work when he is over because I have to babysit two people. I applaud him for trying to help, but I literally cry myself to sleep every night because of the load I have, which no one notices I am carrying. It is more than just having a baby. It is everything else around it. I have to return to a job I don't identify with anymore. I can't take a break because my daughter is watching me. Of course, I feel horrible for saying that."

Journey placed her hands over her eyes and began bawling.

Avery could see the exhaustion in Journey's face—not the exhaustion of someone who hasn't slept—but the exhaustion of someone tired of being strong. Tired of holding everything in. Even when Journey was a little girl, she would empathize with everyone around her and be willing to endure their pain so her loved ones wouldn't feel it. It didn't surprise Avery that Journey had finally cracked. She was feeling her own feelings, and that was so overwhelming that her body could no longer withstand the emotional load of it all.

Avery slid beside Journey on the couch and allowed Journey to cry into her arms. Avery didn't say a word. Journey didn't need any advice; she just needed permission to break.

Later, in an attempt to lighten the mood and offer a suggestion, Avery mentioned a conversation she had with an former client.

"Hey, Journ, have you ever thought about teaching? I had a client who always talked about how much she enjoyed teaching. I hear teachers in New Jersey make really good money, and I am sure you would be more than qualified to teach a civics or law course or something."

Journey cracked a grateful smile. "Yeah, Avery, when I was a kid, I dreamed of being a teacher. But I couldn't imagine being a teacher now."

"Well, I am just putting it out there. I know you said all the other jobs you were looking at didn't pay nearly the same as your attorney salary, but at least if you were in the schools, you could have the summers off with Isabella."

"Hmm, that is a good perk. I appreciate the suggestion, Avery, but I don't know. I will keep looking."

"All right." Avery shrugged her shoulders, her face expressionless.

For a few minutes, neither Avery nor Journey spoke a word. The night had left them speechless and socially exhausted.

Avery eventually broke the silence, "But I gotta go. I have a showing early tomorrow morning."

The two exchanged a hug, and Journey walked Avery out the front door and waited for her to get into her car.

Avery beeped her horn, gave Journey a wave, and then sped down the street. Journey stood there until she could no longer see Avery's vehicle.

After Avery left, Journey felt lonely. She felt empty without a job she loved. It was almost as if all her hard work did not matter. What was life without purpose? Yes, of course, being a mother was the best purpose in the world. But Journey felt she had something inside her that was meant to help people. She did not care about making much money, but she cared about helping many people. How could she do that? Where does one go to find purpose?

The simple answer is God. Whether you'll get your answer immediately is another story, but Journey knew she had to trust in God and continue to pray that He would make a way for her.

Because of how Journey had been feeling over the months, she had stopped attending a physical church but had continued reading the Word at home. It didn't feel the same, but Journey felt she had to stay connected to God somehow.

I know I have to do something drastic for my family. I'm not one to stand around complaining and hating a situation without implementing some action. With consistent prayer, failure, and defeat, I need to go where God leads me. It was clear He no longer wanted me to serve in the role I once did.

CHAPTER 19

The day finally came. Journey looked at herself in the bathroom mirror, expecting her fate to change by freezing in time. However, Journey needed to leave the house soon, or she would have been late for work.

Okay, Journ, you go this. One day at a time. God, please give me strength; I will surely need it.

Mama Luna and Dad arrived at Journey's house just in time for Journey to head out the door.

Dad kissed Journey on the cheek, "Hi, baby! Have a good day at work."

"Hey, Dad," said Journey.

"What's wrong, Journ?" asked Mama Luna.

Journey contemplated revealing everything she felt to her parents but quickly decided not to. Her feelings were between her and God.

"Nothing, Mama. I am just a little tired. Thanks again for watching Isabella while I go back to work. She's asleep in her crib, and her milk and food are in the fridge on the top shelf."

Journey gave her parents a wave and then retreated out the front door.

The drive to the city was one that Journey wasn't used to. She hadn't driven to work in a long time, which was weird. During the car ride, Journey talked to God about returning to work and asked Him for guidance. It was not a short ride and that gave Journey plenty of time to mentally prepare for what awaited her at work.

When Journey arrived at the office, everyone greeted her and expressed how much they had missed her. Although Journey didn't want to be there, it felt nice to be missed. She felt relieved. Journey did not know what to expect, and she was anxious—anxious about starting back to work and being away from Isabella. All the excitement quickly came to a halt. When Journey entered her office, she saw a stack of folders piled on her desk.

Carla entered Journey's office slowly and cautiously. Even after all that time, she wasn't sure where they stood after the fiasco at Lisa and Lance's baby shower. "Hey, Journey, I hoped to catch you before you walked in. We had a few cases routed to you, and they are time-sensitive; I'm sorry."

Although Carla was her assistant, Journey had forgotten that she would have to deal with her. That is how disassociated Journey had been from work.

"Journey?" Carla repeated. "Did you hear me?"

Journey sat down at her desk, distracted. She stuttered, "Oh yes . . . yes, I noticed."

"I know you just got back, but the firm had no other attorney to give the cases to, but since you're the best . . . ," Carla stammered.

Journey quickly interrupted Carla, "I'll do it, don't worry. Forward my calls for the rest of the day."

"Will do," Carla said obediently and left Journey's office.

Although Journey did not want to return to the office or do any of the work given to her, she wasn't lazy. Journey started preparing for the upcoming cases that had been thrown on her desk. She was the last one to leave that night. Or so she thought.

Journey hadn't had time to drop by Joey's office to catch up, and she hadn't been returning his calls or texts about church because she wasn't ready to go back to church. Journey didn't want to face anyone regarding her relationship with God. She was already disappointed in herself and didn't want anyone else to be disappointed.

Journey tried to sneak out the front door, hoping to go undetected. She passed Joey's office in the process, and his face lit up when he saw Journey. She was exhausted and hoped he wouldn't talk to her long.

"Journey! What's going on? How was your first day back?" he asked enthusiastically.

"Exhausting and busy, but it was fine," Journey replied.

"Yeah," Joey said. "I heard they gave you a bunch of new cases. We have all been swamped lately with the increase in business."

"Nice . . . nice." Journey said awkwardly.

Joey cleared his throat. "So, yeah, I'm working on a wrongful conviction suit that has taken up most of my time. I have been working on it for months. I know wrongful conviction cases used to be your favorite."

"Yeah. I always loved a great wrongful conviction case. To bring wrongfully convicted men and women home always gave me so much joy," Journey said remembering those victories.

Joey asked, "But how have you been, Journ? How's Isabella? How are you doing being back?"

Their conversation was interrupted. Journey's phone was ringing.

"Hold on one second, Joey. It's my mom."

"Hey, Journ, when will you be home? Isabella misses her mommy."

"Oh, shoot. Sorry, Ma. I am on my way now."

"No worries, honey. We wanted to make sure you were okay. See you soon."

Journey had texted her parents around four thirty to let them know she would be late coming home. Time slipped away from her, and by the time she was heading out of the office, it was nine o'clock. The ride home would take at least thirty minutes, and Journey felt horrible for making her parents stay that long watching Isabella.

Journey quickly waved goodbye to Joey and raced out of the building. She felt horrible the whole ride home. Journey felt guilty for taking so much of her parents' time. It felt inconsiderate, which Journey was not. She was sure her parents would be annoyed or frustrated with her.

Journey safely sped home and arrived at 9:43 p.m. She ran to the front door, but her father opened it before she could put the key in it.

"Hi, baby," he said excitedly.

"Hi, Dad. I am so sorry," Journey said, out of breath.

"Don't worry about it, sweetheart. We are happy to help," her dad said.

Mama Luna was holding Isabella, and when she spotted her mom walking through the front door, Isabella's eyes lit up.

Seeing Isabella reenergized Journey and instantly made her happy. Nothing else mattered when she stared into Isabella's eyes.

Mama Luna kissed Journey on the cheek and handed Isabella to her; then her parents gathered their belongings and headed home for the night.

"Thank you again!" Journey yelled as she walked her parents out to their car.

Journey placed Isabella in the playpen while she took off her coat and shoes. Then, a knock at the door startled Journey.

"What did you forget, Ma?" Journey laughed as she walked toward the door. When she opened it, there was Lance's face smiling at her.

"What in the world . . . ," Journey was shocked and surprised. She continued, "What are you doing here so late?"

"I'm sorry, Journ. Can I come in?" asked Lance in a chipper tone.

Journey waved Lance inside, but she was confused about why he would decide to show up so late.

"Is everything OK?" Journey asked.

"Yeah, everything is fine," Lance said as he paused and noticed Isabella in the playpen.

"Oh my goodness, is that daddy's baby?" Lance ran to pick Isabella up, and she started giggling. "What are you still doing up?" Lance asked his daughter.

Journey and Lance walked toward the couch while Lance continued to rock and smile at Isabella.

Lance spoke once the two were seated on opposite sides of the couch. "Sorry for coming over so late. I was at a revival service at one of the nearby churches, and I had to come see you."

"Oh my goodness, Lance, that's amazing! Never thought you would be going to church. I know you questioned religion and church and never really bought into it," said Journey.

"I know, right? But I am so glad I went. It was amazing. I felt at peace. I felt free. While I was there, I just started bawling, and I had no idea why."

Journey smiled a grateful smile and added, "That was the presence of God. It's intoxicating."

"It sure was. Better than any drug!" Lance exclaimed.

Journey had spent years trying to get Lance to go to church. Knowing that Lance was doing much better made her feel good.

Lance continued, "I wanted to come here to tell you in person that I gave my life to Christ."

Tears rolled down Journey's face. She was a sucker for redemption stories, and she loved to see people turn to God. Especially Lance. She had always prayed for his soul. The Lance standing before her was different from the one she first met. His soul was nourished, which gave him this attractive glow.

Journey sobbed, "That is amazing to hear, Lance!"

Journey sobbed out of happiness for Lance and sadness for herself. She remembered what it was like to be on fire for the Lord, to go to church, and feel His presence. What happened?

Now that Lance is saved, he is the person I knew he could be. Should we try to work it out and get back together? God, is this a sign?

"Thank you again for never giving up on me, even when I clearly deserved it. Most importantly, thank you for forgiving me. Words cannot express how much you mean to me, Journ. I'm going to heaven because of you," Lance confessed.

Oh my goodness, what am I supposed to say to that?

Journey said a silent thank you to God.

CHAPTER 20

*T*wo *years later.*

Journey had been working on herself deeply. She found some peace in going to therapy, but what had helped her the most were her journal entries. Reflecting on everything she went through and expressing her emotions with pen and paper, she felt free.

Journey picked up her blue ink pen, which glided magically on her journal pages and began her entry.

> *It is going to be a long entry today. It has been a while.*
> *Guess what? I'm married now to a wonderful, God-*
> *fearing man. It has been a different experience, but so*
> *worth it. He was a godsend, and I am honored to be*
> *his wife and the expecting mother of his child. That's*
> *right! I am thirty weeks pregnant with a baby boy!*
>
> *God is the only one who can create life. No one else.*
> *How special it is to have two families join each other*
> *and the miraculous process of blending two ancestral*
> *lines into one child.*

Married life has been amazing. He pays attention to the little things: how I like my tea, the scent of my favorite perfume, and when I am happy or sad. He loves Isabella, and she loves him. That was really important to me. I could never hop into another relationship without making sure Isabella would be comfortable. People say you need time, but I think it depends on the person and where your mind is.

Sometimes, you must do the hard things to reach your blessings. Letting go isn't easy but staying where you don't belong could be detrimental.

I could have easily stayed with Lance, but who's to say history wouldn't repeat itself? It is always tough as a follower of Christ to distinguish when you're meant to forgive someone and stay or forgive them and move on. I had fallen a time or two, but obeying God meant listening to His voice. Obedience is better than sacrifice. His plan for my life was clear. Lance served his purpose in my life, and that lesson was about forgiveness, but having Isabella changed everything for me. For her sake, I knew I couldn't stay.

If I had never given that relationship up and surrendered my life to Christ, I would not be where I am today—an anointed young woman.

I have been at the bottom and thought I could never recover. But the truth is I wouldn't be where I am without my parents and God. I thank God daily for blessing me with parents who introduced me to Him because that allowed me to develop values that I could trust and fall back on.

I can't tell you why we go through the things we go through, but I can say that the journey makes you stronger, and every situation is a lesson, whether you learn from it is another story.

I continued to get closer to God as those around me did: Lance, Nya, and Avery. In addition, my gift got stronger. Nya had a traumatic and scary labor with her little girl, Sophia. But with prayer and petition, Nya got through it and got closer to God. Isabella was so excited to have a little cousin. They're a year apart and inseparable. Zelle and Nya's businesses are growing and stronger than ever. Every weekend we alternate who will host brunch. That has brought all of us closer to each other and God.

The Bible I found in the restaurant that day has been a constant reminder of where I have come from and where I am going. Although I am not the original owner, I'd like to think that it is mine. I don't think it was an accident that I found it. When Isabella is able to read, it can be hers. Hopefully, she finds the right word at the right moment when she needs it.

I guess in the end, I got exactly what I wanted and prayed for. It didn't happen the way I envisioned, but that's because God's ways are higher than our ways, and His thoughts are higher than ours.

"Babe, where are you?"

"I'm in here, babe!" Journey called out.

Journey closed her journal and smiled as her husband walked into the bedroom dressed but missing his tie.

"Oh goodness, you're still not dressed?" Journey laughed. "You are never on time."

"We will be just in time. Your definition of "on time" is being somewhere thirty minutes early," he teased.

"Whatever . . . , Joey," Journey said playfully.

Joey kissed Journey on the forehead and said, "You look beautiful." He placed his hands on her stomach. "How is baby boy doing this morning?"

"Very active," Journey said with a smile.

"Aww, my little athlete. I will meet you and Bella downstairs. Let me grab my tie," he said.

"Okay. Let me wrap up my entry," Journey said determinedly.

"Isabella, come to Mommy's room and bring your church shoes."

Journey reopened her journal and picked up where she left off.

I remember when I was worried about where God would lead me and never could have imagined this new life. When I returned to work after having Isabella I was trying to find myself. I hated what I was doing at the law firm, but the Holy Spirit told me to stay. With every fiber of my being, I wanted to leave, but I kept reminding myself to be obedient. The Holy Spirit told me that God would provide. Of course, at the time it was hard for me to "let go and let God." But God put me in a position where I didn't have a choice.

Shortly after I returned to work, Joey and I got closer. He was a great comfort when I needed it. He reminded me of God's grace, and we started eating lunch together every day—which made work tolerable for me. Then before I knew it, we had been dating for a year when he popped the question. I didn't care to have an elaborate wedding, so we went to the courthouse a couple of months after the engagement. It has been amazing ever since.

Then, the promise God made to me came to pass. The wrongful conviction case that Joey was working on settled, and he received a huge cut of the payout. The right investments enabled me to stop practicing law and focus on another path. I think my next path involves writing. I have fallen in love with it so much. I have so many stories that I want to tell to help inspire my fellow brothers and sisters in Christ.

"Mama, I'm ready!" screamed Isabella.
My baby is calling me; duty calls.

Joey was the Pastor, and Journey was the First Lady at a new and upcoming church close to their home. Every Sunday, they would rush out of the house, no matter how early they woke up. This was a special Sunday—Easter. Churches were always flooded more than usual on Resurrection Sunday.

When Journey and Joey arrived at the church, they parked and went inside. They were both shocked to see that the congregation had grown. Journey decided to sit in the pulpit and let Isabella sit with Nya, her husband Donny, and their daughter Sophia.

Joey and Journey did their meet and greets with some of the visitors and members until church started. The worship team began singing, and Journey observed the congregation. She scanned the room from the pulpit. Journey spotted Nya and her family but didn't immediately see Isabella. She continued scanning the row until she saw Isabella on Lance's lap. A tear dropped onto Journey's cheek. She was so happy and grateful to God. At that moment, everything was worth it. Journey smiled a grateful smile, held her belly, and said quietly to herself, "This was my journey to healing. Who would have thought the healing would be for more than just me? Thank you, God."

ACKNOWLEDGMENTS

All glory and honor to God, who turns hardships into purpose. Writing *Journey* was more than telling a story—it was a testimony of healing, surrender, and trust in God's perfect plan.

To my family, thank you for your unconditional love, prayers, and belief in me even when I doubted myself.

To my loving husband, your encouragement helped carry me through the hardest moments of this process. Thank you for shoring up my confidence with support, faith, and love.

To my editor and everyone who helped shape this book, thank you for your insight, grace, and dedication to the message.

And finally, to every reader who has known heartbreak, disappointment, or the ache of unanswered prayers: This story is for you. May it remind you that God sees, God hears, and He is never finished with your journey.